The Line
by
Louis Orgal

ISBN: 978-0-9874946-1-0

The Line

Gold and trade. The aliens exchanged gold for trade goods at the Line, a line etched north-south across the soil of a continent of a neutral planet. If any human or alien crossed this line to the other side they were killed. If any trader did not meet the specified requirements of their trade goods they were killed.

This high-risk activity employed traders who for a short time were willing to take the risk in return for a lot of gold. But it got very risky when a starting trader took a desperate girl under his wing, and was eventually forced to cross the Line into alien territory, to become a negotiator on the side of the Waps, the alien creatures on the other side of the Line.

Chapter One

"I am here to make money," he thought. The wormhole had deposited him in this solar system. He was now on this planet whose sole physical advantage was that it had a gravity close to Earth's, and was not too hot and not too cold, and an atmosphere, though dry was breathable. Its plant life was limited, and farming possibilities close to zero. Its day was about 25 hours, and orbit stable. But its economic value was almost limitless. Because it was here, only here that the creatures called the Waps, the wasp shaped people, would trade with the humans. Paranoid and belligerent, any further penetration of their space would lead to a manic attack. Few survived the encounter. But here on this planet, located at the very limits of their empire or sphere of settlement, whatever you liked to call it, they were willing to trade. This was the Line.

The wormholes through which ships travelled were randomly distributed. Some solar systems had many wormholes, some had few, but they were the only feasible way to travel from star to star in a person's lifetime.

Their physics was little understood. Exploration for new wormholes was ongoing, but it gradually became clear that whole sections of the galaxy could be accessed by only one or two wormholes. Some sections indeed could not yet be accessed at all.

The wasp creatures' area could be accessed by only one wormhole. Early explorers quickly found that they were not friendly, and for many years they were left alone. But human curiosity never ends, and by a dint of many trials it was found that they were willing to trade in a limited fashion. After much trial and error it was found that what they had to sell was pharmaceutical gold, life and intelligence enhancing drugs. And what these creatures wanted in return, and what they had an insatiable desire for, was tea and coffee. So trade relations were set up.

But where? The only place was this planet in the 'Pinch'. The solar system where two wormholes met, each wormhole leading to either human or Waps space. This solar system was useless to either side except for this anomaly. Yes, the planet had an atmosphere breathable for humans and apparently the Waps. So the humans and the Waps met together to trade.

But trading was not simple. If the human ships got too near to the Waps they were shot at. The only safe place for them to land was on the opposite side of the globe to the Waps domicile, and the ships had to carefully land and take off without orbiting over the Waps settlement, otherwise they would be fired upon with occasional fatal consequences. Similarly human ships had to stay well clear of Waps ships. Fortunately the Waps had the same attitude.

Trade was at the "Line", a line drawn North-South across a continent and half way between the Waps and human space ports, which were many thousand kilometres away from each other. The Line was quite literally drawn on the ground by some sort of laser device. Any human crossing the Line, sometimes even leaning over, died. The Waps in turn never attempted to cross the line to the human side.

And what a line! By mutual consent, there was a middle point of the line at the equator. To the north of the equator the humans sold their goods in return for bars of gold. To the south of the equator the humans bought what the Waps had to sell for bars of gold. At the equator was a gold exchange on the human side of the line, where gold bars were bought and sold for money. Waps would only buy and sell for gold bars. Yes genuine gold. Of an agreed weight and purity. You bought the gold at the gold exchange at the centre of the town, at the equator, with Credits, and when you received bars of gold for what you sold, you exchanged them for Credits.

Near the equator both the humans and Waps built a string of buildings facing the line. Trading firms that sold and bought standardised goods at more or less standard prices possessed each of the buildings. A large-scale transfer of goods occurred each way. Essentially mass production. Further away from the equator the buildings began to peter out into more temporary buildings, and then tents, and eventually hopeful individuals waiting at the line to trade. Waps always turned up to look at what you had. Sometimes you could be lucky...

A road paralleled the Line north and south. At the equator it was a major multilaned highway, but it deteriorated the further you went from the town, and ended up as an unsurfaced track. At the equator was a city, called the Line, built in a grid pattern, with all the normal services and a large population. The only distinction to any other human city was that all the buildings were one story. Any attempts to build higher were shot at.

During trading no cheating was allowed. This rule was rigidly enforced. The penalty for even inadvertent error was death. If your goods did not meet specification, the Waps insisted and invariably had the trader returned to the 'court house' at the Line at the equator, and after it was found that the goods did not meet quality or quantity agreed, their own side executed the person. A blast from a gun. The Waps did it to their own too.

The consequences were nasty if this was not done. A sector of buildings around the offending trading house was levelled. The humans quickly learned to enforce this rule. But the rule was enforced on the Waps side too. A Waps was duly delivered for trial, and if found guilty, executed. But this did not prevent the Waps trying to cheat from time to time. The humans found it necessary to enforce this rule on the Waps, or cheating and bad deliveries would escalate. This was the only way contracts could be enforced.

As a consequence the role of trader employed by the trading houses was not a popular one, especially as they sometimes did not have control over the quality of the goods delivered. Some trading houses had a habit of sometimes being a bit short on quality or quantity according to the specifications required by the Waps, and the unfortunate trader had to pay with his life. Naturally people who were willing to be traders on the sell side were hard to find, difficult to hold onto for any length of time, and had to be paid very well indeed.

Buying traders had a different problem. Though they just delivered gold, and purchased the goods; the Waps did not seem to have any scruples on cheating if the could possibly get away with it. Yes, they delivered a Waps to be executed, and trading houses soon learned not to have any scruples in insisting that this be done, but a good buying trader learned to check for quality on the spot. Soon the Waps learned which traders they could not cheat.

But, John Griffin, for that was his name, had applied for the job of selling trader. He was a gambler. He knew that if he lasted six months and was not stiffed by his firm, Albrecht and Co, he would make a million credits. They would pay him, or his estate, regardless, pro rata for the number of days he lasted. But they would only pay at the end of the contract, or his death. They had too many people running off.

They swore that they had quality checks, and there would be no mistakes. His predecessor had lasted six months and was about to leave. But the problem of continuously monitoring a commodity such as tea or coffee was next to impossible. If the firm raised the quality for safety's sake they would lose money. If they lowered it closer to the minimum required, statistical variation would get you…..

John was sure that the firm had no concern for him personally, had coldly done the calculation of the cost and inconvenience of replacing him, and estimated the probable cost against the likely gain from lowering the quality. All within a six month period…."The last three months will be hell," John thought. "I shall be a sunk cost to the firm. They can stiff me in the last few days and make money!"

The trip to the line from the spaceport city was now on a well-constructed freeway. No flying vehicles were allowed. A stream of trucks accompanied the coach he was in at 300 kph, and there was a stream of trucks coming the other way. "All to keep those billions in the galaxy alive and healthy" he thought. "It would be highly profitable if it was a monopoly". But of course it was not. For a brief period it was. The "John Company" made quadrillions and had set up the system, but political pressure from thousands of planets and sheer greed had forced others in. It was now a "level playing field", so it was said. But that was nonsense. The big companies had trading buildings at the core, with conveyor belts, and continuous non-stop buying and selling, while small traders were forced far to the north and south, where there was just a line burnt in the soil. There they stood and waited with their goods or gold, but even out there Waps turned up to trade. "The market is universal", John thought, "Adam Smith was right." Of course the traders out there had to experiment buying and selling new products to make a buck. They could not compete with the standard products. And if you found a new bonanza…You quickly set up a tent next to the long line of shacks, and with your new found 'friends' bought and sold like mad until the firms further down the line moved in. But there was such a multiplicity of goods now changing hands/talons there was a chance that competition could be staved off for a while.

"If I last six months and get my million, that is what I will do", John was thinking to himself when the coach suddenly decelerated, curved around a giant circle at the end of the freeway, and entered a coach station. He got out, claimed his luggage, and glanced at the bit of paper with the address of the office he was supposed to go to. "Corner of Third Avenue and North Second Street. Nice and central. I will just walk there" he thought, and picked up his bags.

He found the shiny office of Albrecht and Company and went in. He saw the receptionist inside a not very large hallway and went up and said, "I have an appointment to see Mr Walker". The girl looked up and gave him a strange look. "Who shall I say it is?" "John Griffin". The girls leant down and spoke into a phone, and a few moments later a cheery man came out of a door at the end of the hall.

"John Griffin. Come in. Come in. I've been expecting you. Come along to my office!" and he swept John into his office.

"So you are to become one of our new traders," he exclaimed. "You have no doubt taken the training course. Learnt the language, though of course the translator will assist you. Learnt the trading techniques. What is expected of you. Well, I shall have you taken to your accommodation, and you can start tomorrow".

"Won't I be given some sort of induction? A training period?" John asked.

"Of course. Of course. One of our managers will give you the run down. But unfortunately your predecessor, well you know how it is, had an accident. Most unfortunate. A difference of opinion over the quality of some tea. I was at the trial this morning. Most unfortunate. But nothing could be done. The fault was clear, and the Waps trader insisted! "

"You mean he was executed!"

"Yes, very sad, but painlessly I assure you. And quick. We now have a professional who does this sort of thing. But I am sure it won't happen to you! It happens only very occasionally, with our firm at least. But we need someone else to start as soon as possible. A big opportunity for you! You can start trading straight away! You will find it amazingly simple, and the Waps you deal with are very cooperative. Now if you step this way I shall have you taken to your accommodation." He was already ushering John out of the office. "Stephne" he said, turning to the girl at the counter "Can you call a cab for John, and give him a taxi coupon, a card for expenses, and tell him where to go." With that the man shook John's hand, and swept back to his office.

Stephne gave John another strange look, and called a cab. "Here is the taxi charge coupon and an expenses card, and here is the address. It is a group of small apartments. Just tell the manager at the front office who you are. I shall let him know. Your expense money will be paid weekly in advance into your account. And best of luck!" She smiled and looked as if she meant it.

Chapter Two

The set of ground floor apartments were not far away, but further from the Line. Just a single room with a bed, with kitchen facilities and a separate bathroom, set around an internal courtyard.

John unpacked his things, and then left the room, and walked to the reception to enquire about somewhere to eat. He was told that there was a small restaurant bar down the street, and he stepped out into the warm sunshine and walked down the block.

He soon reached the bar, which he saw offered some basic eats. "I shall have to cook for myself if this is all I get" he thought to himself. He sat down at a table and was approached by a rather attractive blonde waitress.

She handed him a menu and smiled, "Would you like a drink?". "A beer please". He looked at her as she retreated to the bar. "Hmm," he thought. She soon returned with the beer. "Have you thought what you want?" "I'll have soy-steak and salad please". She walked back to the bar.

Just at that point a male walked into the restaurant, walked up to the waitress and grabbed her. "Let go of me!" she squealed. "What have you been doing?" the male asked. She replied, "I told you, I don't want to see you again!" "Oh yeah" the man replied, and slapped her across the face. The girl screamed. Then John noticed that no one in the bar would come to the girl's rescue. The other customers looked away, and the barkeep disappeared. The girl struggled and screamed. John leapt to his feet. "Hey!" he yelled, and approached the assailant. The guy looked at him and said, "You keep out of this!" he said and produced a device that projected a thin vibrating blade. Without thinking, John leapt behind him, grabbed the arm, twisted it around and broke it. The man yelled, swore, and grabbed into his pocket for something else. John quickly jabbed him in his solar plexus with the stiffened point of his fingers. The man collapsed.

"So my martial arts training works," John thought to himself. He then pulled out his mobile phone and called the police.

The police interviewed him and took a statement, all the time looking at him closely. He had to ring his employer, and eventually Mr Walker turned up, looking harassed. "What on earth did you do? Getting yourself in trouble immediately after you have arrived? Come with me. I'll take you back to the hotel. I have squared things with the police."

Mr Walker took John back to the hotel in his vehicle. "Stay here. If you need to eat send out for it. I shall see you tomorrow back at the office."

The next day, in his office, Mr Walker did not look too pleased. "OK, no-one will harm you as long as you continue to work for this company. You have beaten up the son of a local criminal, but they see that he acted foolishly and you had no premeditation. I have settled things. But stay out of trouble from now on! If we didn't need you, we wouldn't be going to this trouble for you. Now I shall take you to your trading station". He sighed, picked up his car keys, and ushered John into his vehicle.

The trade station was a long open ended building adjoining others, facing the road. Trucks backed in one end of the building, the other end of which faced the Line, and opened into another building on the other side of the line.

There were a number of people in the building, some handling machines mainly unloading and loading chest of tea and bags of coffee on and off the trucks, supervisors with clip-boards, armed guards, and a manager. The building smelled of tea and coffee.

"Here, put this on", Mr Walker said. It was a green iridescent jacket with a shiny surface. "This is a trader's jacket. Come and meet the temporary trader, Jim Stevens. He will show you the ropes, and introduce you to your Waps opposite number."

"Jim!" Mr Walker yelled, "Here is the new trader, John Griffin".

A white haired and pale man, also wearing a green jacket, turned around and smiled. "Hi", he said, "welcome to the circus. I hope you have been trained. But it is not very hard. The prices are pretty standard. It is just a matter of counting. You have to be exact with that. Especially the gold bars. But remember your own life depends on the quantity of goods coming from our side. And of course the quality. I shall show you how to sample," and he gave Mr Walker a look, "We have this device with which the signals penetrates right to the centre of the consignments. But you have to keep it calibrated – that's your job".

Mr Walker protested, "We never knowingly reduce quality!". Jim ignored him. Jim pointed at a white line engraved into the floor. "That is the Line. Don't go over it. Don't even put any part of you body over it. You may get away with it. You may not. But remember the penalty is death if you don't!"

John looked around. Everybody else was standing meters away, including Mr Walker who was backing away. "See that green line?" said John, pointing to another line three meters back, "Nobody else but you is advised to cross that line, and they try not to do it. Everybody has great respect for the Waps." The conveyor was thirty meters in length. While it could be loaded at any point, all the staff congregated at the end. Nobody liked to approach the green line.

"So come along and meet the Waps."

The creature towered above him, calmly looking down on him from multi-faceted eyes. There were four arms attached to a hard dark blue thorax. Each hand at three fingers at its end. One hand carried a device. Jim picked up a translator device and attached it to his garment, and attached a microphone to his head. He calmly spoke into it. A kind of warble and chirp emitted from the speaker.

Without preliminaries Jim said, "May I introduce your new trader."

The Waps bowed slightly and warbled in reply, "He is welcome. I look forward to working with him for a long time." John heard a warbling sound issuing from around the wing space of the Waps, but the words came out of a speaker on the front of his thorax.

"Here", said Jim, "Put one of these on. Do you know how to use it?"

"Yes" John replied, and attached the translator to himself, "What do I do now?"

The translator immediately translated these words. The Waps seem to chuckle.

The Waps began talking. The sound issued from a speaker attached to the front of its thorax. "It is simple. The system has been worked out over a long period of time. I do not understand why there are occasional mistakes. I believe that your predecessor did not intend to cheat. But I had to enforce the rules. With the agreement of your associate I shall explain what I expect to be the rules".

Jim said, "I agree".

"Confirmed. At this location we exchange cases of tea and bags of coffee, each of standard weight, for bars of gold of standard weight and quality. The price varies slightly with the stated quality of tea and coffee. I do not know what your preferences are, but for our purposes, we prefer certain types of tea and coffee, and are willing to pay less or more for these different types of tea and coffee as a consequence. These prices have been agreed prior to your arrival, and if we wish to change them we shall inform you. From our experience, you will then inform your own people that a price change has been requested, and another person appears to negotiate with us."

The Waps stopped and looked at him, and continued.

"You have two roles. First count the boxes of tea and coffee proceeding over the Line, and the gold bars coming over the line in the other direction. At any point in time the transfer is not directly comparable. We have agreed with your people that we run up what you call a credit, and then at a certain time, we transfer nearly all the gold bars we owe you. The equipment transferring the gold bars is somewhat different to that transferring the tea and coffee. The gold is transferred in stacks of bars. You have to check the quantity, weight and quality of the gold crossing the line and inform us if there is a discrepancy."

"Your second role, and the more important one from both our points of view," and at this point the Waps seemed to give a chuckle, "You have to check the quality of the tea and coffee before it crosses the line. Every chest of tea, every bag of coffee. It is your personal responsibility, on which our life depends."

At this point the Waps turned to Jim and asked. "Have I been correct in everything I have said?"

Jim replied, "Yes, you have." Jim then turned to John without further courtesies to the Waps, "I shall fill in the rest."

"On each chest of tea and bag of coffee is marked a code name. This name is the code name for the quality of the parcel of tea or coffee. This gizmo, and this is mine, though you will get one too, will check the quality of the tea or coffee. It is in effect a form of radar. Just point it at the case or bag, set the code on the device, and it should confirm that the quality is correct, and also the weight in the case or bag."

"What if it isn't?" John asked.

"Just send it back. Sometimes they will argue. My advice is to carry a paint marker with you always. Just mark the offending case or bag which is below par and send it back. It never seems to be above par. They don't like it, but remember it is your life".

"Where do I get one of these devices?"

"They should give you one now. But remember calibrate it always before you start each day. They have sample packages to calibrate it on near the entrance. But I found that is always a good idea to pop into neighbouring firms early in the morning to check your calibration. The trader there will allow you. We try to stick together." And Jim winked.

Jim turned to the Waps. "If you will excuse us. I am getting John a calibration machine. We will be back shortly".

The Waps hummed and said. "I will allow John to get his calibration machine."

They walked back to the entrance of the building. John noticed that the conveyor belt was already stacked with cases of tea, ready to roll. Mr

Walker stood there holding the device, and handed it to John.

Jim said, "Now I shall show you the samples. They are supposed to be kept in good order." He pointed to a shelf with a line of labelled glass jars. "Have you had training using this?" "Yes" John replied. He proceeded to point the device it each glass jar one by one, typing in the codes as shown on the jars. Each time the device gave a plangent tone and flashed a green light. Suddenly there was a buzz and the device flashed red. Jim, Mr Walker and the entire crew watching froze. Jim looked Mr Walker in the eye, without saying a word.

Mr Walker recovered quickly. "Hah, I see you have found our test sample! This to show you that the device works. Now where is the correct sample?" And he hurried around to a desk, looked around underneath it, and dragged out another jar.

"Try that!" he said smiling. There was a correct response from the device.

"OK" said Jim "I will be with you for a couple of hours. We will both check each consignment with both our devices. This will make sure that there are no mistakes."

With that, after finishing checking the rest of the samples, they went back to the line.

On the way back Jim said, "Also check to see if the weight sampler is working by checking against several of the waiting cases and bags. They should show the same weights to point one per cent accuracy".

"See here. Here is the first consignment." John looked at the chest of tea waiting in the conveyor belt to slide across the line to the Waps conveyor belt. "While the accounting is done automatically I consider it a good idea for you to do two things. Keep a notebook and note each consignment as you check the quality with the machine. Then you sing out to the Waps. "One case of tea. Such and such a quality. See on this display is the price. Such and such grams of gold. The Waps will say "Acknowledge". And you press the button and the case slides over the line. Understood?"

"Yes", said John, ""It sounds simple enough."

"It does, but remember you are trading with your life. Stay alert at all times! Now lets see how you do it. Now where's some paper?" And he rooted around under the console, and dug up an account book and a pen. In it was neatly written a list of transactions. Type, quantity, quality and price. The last entry was dated the day before yesterday. Jim grimaced. "This will do," he said, as he turned to a fresh page. "Now lets see how you go."

John looked at the waiting chest of tea, and fed into the testing device the quality code on the side.

"Don't hurry", Jim said. John pressed the test button. A plangent tone sounded and the device showed green. "Fill in the book," Jim said. "Tea, 500 kilos, PK49, 825 grams of gold".

"Excellent" said Jim, "Now read it out in a loud voice".

John looked at the Waps, and said. "Tea, 500 kilos, quality PK49, 825 grams of gold".

John waited. The Waps looked at what appeared to be a kind of reader. "Confirmed" the voice from the transponder said.

"Press the green button" Jim said. John pressed the button. The case slid forward, landed on the Waps' conveyor belt, and then slid forwards a short distance. The Waps produced a device and pressed it against the case. "Product, quantity and quality confirmed. Price agreed." announced the Waps. Jim looked relieved. "You didn't tell me about this, Jim," John said. "I didn't want to worry you. If you get too stressed you make mistakes. Now how are you going? Do you want to do the next one?"

The next couple of hours proceeded uneventfully, even boringly. The cases of tea were replaced by bags of coffee. The gold credit account crept up. Jim stayed around, though he plainly wanted to go. Then it was announced that it was time for a gold delivery.

"We do this normally when we are owed 500 kilos of gold. We don't like amounts over this to accumulate."

He turned to the Waps. "We would like a delivery of 500 kilos of gold."

"Confirmed" said the Waps.

Jim shouted back along the building to the entrance "Gold delivery!".

Immediately the atmosphere in the building changed. The conveyor reversed and the cases and bags were taken off it. The security guards became much more in evidence.

The Waps said, "Here is the gold". And yes, there was a pile of gold bars on the conveyor belt.

The Waps placed his device against the pile. "One hundred kilograms of 99.99 per cent pure gold".

"Confirmed" said Jim, and said to John "Write in your book 100 kilograms of 99.99 per cent pure gold".

The conveyor moved, moved the gold across the Line, and deposited the gold on their conveyor.

"Press your device onto the gold and press the gold button," Jim said. The machine said "100 kilograms of gold 99.99 per cent pure". Jim shouted "Product, quantity and quality confirmed" and pressed the red button on the conveyor. The conveyor reversed and took the gold to the end of the building. Jim noticed that they were all 10 kilo gold bars.

Jim said, "You have a go". John turned and saw another pile of gold bars waiting at the end of the Waps' conveyor. The Waps announced "One hundred kilograms of 99.99 per cent pure gold ".

John said "Confirmed" and wrote it in his book. The gold moved across the line. John pressed the gold button on his machine and pressed it against the pile of gold. The machine said "100 kilograms of gold 99.99 per cent pure."

John shouted "Product, quantity and quality confirmed" and pressed the red button. The gold disappeared down to the other end, and John turned to process the next pile of gold.

After they had processed 500 kilograms of gold, Jim shouted to the other end "Gold delivery completed" and then turned to John. "Well, that's the entire process. Do you think you can manage from now on?"

"Sure".

Jim shook his hand, and looking relieved, began to turn and walk away.

"I just got one question," John said, "What about lunch, breaks and going to the toilet?"

"Oh, you can stop any time. They don't like it, but you should take regular rest breaks. There is a small incentive system to keep the stuff rolling. It is fed into your expense account. It adds up. But don't overdo it. The Waps also disappears from time to time. It helps if you coincide. And oh yes, you have to bring a packed lunch and refreshments in with you. You can pop across the road to get something today. And the toilets are at the end."

With that, Jim turned and hurried off.

Chapter Three

The rest of the day was uneventful though stressful. At the end of the day, all the cases of tea and bags of coffee had been delivered and another credit of gold had been accumulated but not delivered. It seemed everybody was happy to pack it in.

John looked at his measuring device and decided to take it home with him. The manager Mr Walker was there. He seemed happy. "Early start tomorrow, John. We like to start at 8 am."

John set off for his apartment. On his way he saw a supermarket, and remembered Jim's words about a packed lunch. He ducked in, grabbed a trolley, and began to load it with edibles. "I suppose I had better grab stuff for a breakfast, cereals, coffee, tea, milk" he thought, and piled it all in with self-heating lunches and assorted breads and spreads.

After paying, he had two heavy bags of food. He put his measuring device in one bag and set off for his accommodation. And ran into a group of toughs. There was mutual recognition. One of the guys had an arm in a sling and gave John a vicious look. John stopped and looked around. It seemed as if there was no help and nowhere to go. The guy showed his teeth and said "It's you again" and stepped forward. It was clear what his intention was, even with one arm in a sling.

Friends on either side of him grabbed his arm and said "Come on. Leave him alone". They pulled the guy past John. The guy's last words were "I'm going to get you. Just you wait!" John turned to watch then walk down the street.

On reaching his room, John prepared a meal, had a shower, and got ready for bed. He was a lot more tired than he first thought he was.

Suddenly he felt a light tap on his door. "Who's there?" he asked. There was another tap. John went up to the door and said, "Who's that?" There was a pause and then a girl's voice "Please let me in."

John opened the door a crack. It was the blonde girl at the restaurant. "What? What do you want?" he said.

The girl looked up an down the corridor and whispered, "Please can I come in?"

Dumbfounded, John opened the door. The girl quickly entered, and turned round to close the door.

"They are after me! I had nowhere else to go! All my friends have been questioned. I thought you could put me up for the night."

"Why?"

"You saved me from Rick. Everybody is afraid of him. Or his Dad. I can stay here for a night, then get back to Spaceport when the fuss has died down."

"Why me?" John asked.

"I'll be safe here. Nobody will touch you as you work for the company. They won't look here. Oh, please, please, please! You are my only chance! Rick is threatening to cut me up. He blames me for what happened. He can do it! No one will stop him! Oh, please! You can't make me go. He will kill me!" The girl then burst into tears and flung herself at John.

John put his arms around her. He temporized. "How did you find out where I was?" he asked. "I have a friend who works for the hotel" she replied, and began sobbing uncontrollably.

"Oh, all right, you can spend the night here."

"Oh thank you, thank you, thank you! You have saved my life!" She grabbed his hands and kissed them, still sobbing.

"Well, sit down. Have you eaten anything?"

"Not much," she sniffled, "I have been trying to stay out of sight."

"I have got some food." He began to un-pack the bags. "What would you like?"

She selected a self-heating stew and scoffed it. She obviously had not eaten for a day. John ate pasta a bit more slowly. "Coffee?" John asked. He heated up some water, broke open some sachets, opened a half-liter carton of milk, and looked in the cupboard for cups. It was well stocked. "I could take a bowl in and have breakfast at work," he thought, "if I am late".

After coffee, the sleeping arrangements had to be decided. It was a standard double bed. John briefly considered sleeping on the floor, but decided it was silly. They would both share the bed, but he was not going to ask for sex. For a start, he did not know the girl. Also he was much too tired.

He set the alarm for 6.30 leaving half an hour to walk to work, and said to the girl "Which side of the bed do you want?"

"I don't mind."

"I will sleep next to the door".

They both got undressed. John put on his nightwear and washed his teeth while the girl quickly reduced her clothes to her undergarments and climbed into bed.

John turned off the lights, turned on his side, said good night, and immediately dropped into a deep sleep.

To be woken up next morning by the alarm. The girl was wrapped around him with her arm around his chest. He thought, "If I knew this, I would not have gone to sleep so soon." He hopped out of bed and did his ablutions while the girl lay in bed half asleep.

Then a thought occurred to him – the cleaner! "You can't stay here" he said, "The cleaner will find you."

That woke her up. "Oh, what am I going to do?" she asked, her hand at her mouth.

"Well, you can't stay here. The hotel management will certainly throw you out, and probably inform the crims as well. Get dressed and I shall think about it. And I have got to go to work pretty soon."

Then a thought struck him. "The only safe place for you is at my workplace, when you are with me. The crims can't touch me, and they won't touch you while you are with me. You will have to come with me to work, and come back to stay with me at the hotel for a few nights until you can make your escape."

"You sure?"

"Yes, I can't be in any worse trouble with the company than at present. They will just have to put up with me until they can replace me." He didn't say how they would replace him.

After the girl had dressed he noticed that they were running out of time. "We need to get moving now to get there on time. We shall eat breakfast and lunch at work. Grab a couple of bowls, spoons, cereal and milk, and packets of lunch."

On the way John asked, "I don't know your name."

"Call me Gwen," was the reply, "Short for Gwendolyn. That is what I was named at birth, but I have never used that name!" she giggled nervously. "I'm John," John said.

On arrival, John announced, "I have got myself an assistant. She will be with me beyond the green line".

Everyone's eyes opened. The manager perked up, "You can't do that! That's not allowed!"

"I don't see why not. You are not paying her anything. She will stay with me and assist with the work. She will be no trouble."

With that, John swept the girl around them and up past the green line.

He heard a loud discussion behind him. The conveyor did not start rolling. There seemed to be some sort of hiatus.

The Waps was ready and waiting. John introduced her to him.

"Here is my new assistant. Her name is Gwen. She will help with the procedure. I hope that when she is trained we can speed the process up."

The Waps bowed slightly. "Welcome Gwen. This is the first time the human trader has had an assistant." There was a pause. "I notice that this person is physically different from you. May I ask why?"

"She is a female of our species."

There was a strange buzzing sound from the Waps, not translated by the translator. Then there was silence for a few seconds. Then another question. "May I ask, is she your mate?"

John drew his breath. "No she is not. We have no sexual relationship. We are just friends." John heard a low giggle next to him.

To this, the Waps did not reply, but just stood and observed both of them.

In the meantime, nothing was happening further back, except loud talk. "I think we had better have some breakfast," John announced. He reached into the bag and handed one of the bowls to Gwen. "Krispies and milk?" "Yes, please," Gwen replied. John poured in a bowl of Krispies and poured in some milk, and did the same for himself. They began to eat.

After a while they noticed that the Waps seemed to get agitated. "Oh dear, we are upsetting the Waps. Put the bowls down. We'll eat later."

Just after that Mr Walker appeared. He looked flushed and angry. "Who is this?" he shouted.

"She is my assistant," John replied.

"Well she can't work here!"

"Yes she can. She is working for me. You are not paying her anything."

"If she is not gone immediately I shall fire you!"

"Fine. But I am well aware that you cannot replace me for three months. That is how long you have before you can train a replacement. Do you want that?"

Mr Walker went bright red and shouted, "You will hear about this! You will regret this!" and began to turn away.

"One last thing," John said, "She is wanted by those criminals who tried to kill me. If anything happens to her I shall cease to work for you."

"Wahat!" screamed Mr Walker, "I can't protect her! You're mad!"

"You'd better. Think of all the money you would lose. I estimate it about a million dollars a day."

Mr Walker went pale and his jaw quivered. He gave John a vicious look into his eyes and walked away.

Gwen asked, "Do you mean that?"

"Yes," replied John, "They have to keep me alive and operating for up to three months. You will be safe until then."

"What will happen after that?"

"Then they will try to kill me."

"Kill you! How?"

"They will make a mistake with a consignment, and let the Waps do it."

"Oh no! I can't let them do that! I'd better go!"

"No, you can't. The crims will be waiting for you. You won't last a minute. Stay with me, and I will get you on that ship."

"But what about you?"

"I'll think about something. Don't worry." John did not feel at all confident.

The Waps was standing there watching them. But his calm demeanor seemed to have gone.

"May I make a request?" the Waps said.

"Yes, sure."

"I am interested in the contents of those bowls. May I see them?"

John was surprised. Everything seemed to be happening at once.

"Yeah, sure" he said, looking around for a way of handing the Waps a bowl without endangering himself.

At that moment the conveyor belt cranked up and the first case appeared. "I will place the bowl just in front of the case, and you will get it with the case," John said. The Waps eyed the bowl and said nothing.

John turned to Gwen and said, "Watch me. It's simple and routine. But on your life, you had better be accurate and one hundred per cent on the ball!"

With that he picked the testing device out of the bag, switched it on, and thought "Here goes!"

He saw it was a case of tea, 500 kilos, PK72 grade, 864 grams price according to the readout. He wrote this down in the book, pressed the device on the case that pinged and flashed green, and announced "Tea, 500 kilograms, grade PK72, price 864 grams".

The Waps said "Acknowledged", but gave John a strange look.

John quickly poured both bowls of milk and cereal into one bowl and placed it on the conveyor in front of the case of tea, and pressed the green button. Both the case and bowl proceeded over the line, not spilling.

No person at the rear had noticed this transaction. They were too busy placing cases on the conveyor.

The Waps placed his device on the case and announced "Product, quantity and quality confirmed. Price agreed." And then said "What price would you like for the other product?" John replied, "Don't worry. It is a free sample. A present from me."

The Waps looked at him and said, "Confirmed" and a companion appeared to take the bowl.

The rest of the day went without a hitch. Indeed Gwen did prove useful, taking over the writing in the book. The processing speeded up. "I am adding to my expenses bonus," John thought. "This is working well".

With a pleasant companion, the rest of the day proceeded speedily. In fact John got in two gold deliveries.

They eventually ran out of deliveries, and John noticed that the staff quickly left.

Walking to the end, he noticed that there was a reception committee waiting for him.

Chapter Four

"That's her!" a voice said. He saw it was Rick, next to an older man and a number of tough looking companions. "Grab her!"

John pulled Gwen back behind him. "As I explained to Mr Walker, if anything happens to her, I will cease working for the company!"

"As if I give a fuck!" shouted Rick, trying to grab Gwen. John pulled her further back, inside the building. John then noticed a group of tough looking security guards behind him, who stepped up, gripping their weapons. The mob stepped back.

From behind the mob of crims stepped Mr Walker. "Griffin!" he shouted, "Let the girl go! It would be better for you! You are in a lot of trouble! Just let these people have her!"

"No!" shouted John, "As I told you, if anything happens to the girl, anything at all, I shall cease working for you. That means today, tonight, at the hotel, anytime. If a hair is touched on her head you will have to find a new trader."

Mr Walker's face twisted and his mouth worked up and down, while his eyes rotated. He looked as if sweat had penetrated through his suit so that it looked dark and soaking.

Mr Walker was about to say something, and then suddenly grabbed Rick's older companion and dragged him away. There was an earnest conversation, with Mr Walker arguing intensely. Eventually they all, including Mr Walker, walked away.

"Well, it looks as if we are free to go," said John, holding Gwen and beginning to walk.

"Are you sure?" said Gwen.

"Yes." Said John, "I have called their bluff. Whoever the criminals are they do not want to upset the company. You will be safe for the time being. On the way back we had better pop into a supermarket. Both of us need to eat. We can get you some toiletries and things. And we can get some more milk." An idea was beginning to form….

They entered a supermarket, and John seized a trolley. They then proceeded around make purchases. "Why are you buying so much milk?" Gen asked as he began stacking several liter cartons into the trolley.

"I like it," was John's only reply. He added some extra packets of Krispies. "I am a breakfast freak."

When they reached the hotel, there was another altercation with the hotel manager. "She can't stay here!"

"Why not?"

"She's not booked in!"

"She's staying in my room."

"That will cost extra. The company did not inform us that she is staying, and has not paid for her."

"I will pay for her."

"This is most irregular!"

"Look, if there is any nonsense about her staying I shall inform Mr Walker. She is staying in my room as long as she likes." And with that John walked up the corridor, holding Gwen's hand. John turned around and shouted, "And if there is any nonsense at all, such as visitors I don't like, I shall complain to Mr Walker. You understand? And oh, yes, I shall require a key card for the lady. I shall collect it on the way out tomorrow."

The door opened without trouble and John and Gwen entered the room. It looked as if the room had been cleaned, and then entered again, and his belongings searched, but nothing was gone. "Hmmm," I suppose worse could have happened he thought.

"Dinner?" he asked.

The night was uneventful and he slept like a log.

Arriving near the workplace next day, John popped into the firm next door. "Can I test my device against your samples?" he asked.

A man replied, "You are the guy next door. Go ahead. You've caused quite a commotion. I don't know how long you are going to last." They all looked at him in wonder.

"I intend to last a long time," John said. There were chuckles around the room.

Heading next door to Albrecht and Company, John and Gwen were greeted by stunned silence.

"Fire her up! We don't have time to waste!" he shouted, and they walked to the end past the green line.

"Greetings" said John to the waiting Waps, pulling a liter of milk out of his bag and putting it on the ground near the end of the conveyer belt, as if he was getting ready for breakfast.

The Waps said, "I am glad you have arrived," eying the milk.

"Let it roll," shouted John to the men at the other end, and soon the first case arrived.

He said quietly to Gwen "Stand just here so they can't see what I am doing." She moved to block the view.

"Tea, 500 kilograms, grade PT14, price 851 grams", and he placed the liter of milk and a packet of Krispies on the end of the conveyor before pressing the green button.

The Waps purchased the tea, and then picked up the milk. "What price do you want for this?"

"You make an offer," said John, fully intending to accept whatever was offered. "That will be the standard volume of delivery, in that package." John and Gwen stood side-by-side blocking the view from further down the room.

"Understood. I do not need the other solid."

"Keep it. It is free."

The rest of the day was uneventful. The boxes and bags were dispatched and sold, and gold was received in payment.

That night they returned straight to the hotel. John had enough milk in the fridge.

The hotel manager eyed them but did not say a word. The room was untouched.

"I think we are out of trouble for the moment," John said, but rolled his eyes and touched his lips. She immediately understood. "We had better have something to eat."

The next day, before they entered their trade building they popped next door to check the device; "You are still alive, huh?" was the wry comment. They then walked next door and through the silent workers to the Line.

The Waps was waiting for them. "I offer one kilo of gold for that quantity of liquid".

"I call it a liter of milk. The offer is accepted. With two provisos."

"What are those?"

"First. The milk is my own property. I request that the amount of gold paid for this milk to be paid into a separate credit account in my own name. Do you understand that?"

After a moments hesitation the Waps said, "Yes. Agreed. What is the second request?"

"The second request is that when there is a deficiency in the value of any product delivered to you by my firm, you deduct the value of the deficiency from my credit balance, and do not ask for my death."

There was a moment's silence. Then a sort of chuckle. Then the Waps said "Agreed."

Then the first case of tea arrived.

John said to Gwen "Move there", pointing to a spot obstructing the view to the men at the end, and placed a liter of milk in front of the case. He then went through the process checking the consignment and transferred it to the Waps.

The Waps confirmed the consignment of tea. Then said "One liter of milk. Price one kilo of gold. Credited to John."

John said immediately "There is a third proviso. Do not verbally confirm the sale of the milk. I shall trust you."

"Agreed."

"Phew. That is a weight off my shoulders. They will find it difficult to kill me now!" But he had forgotten to turn his translator off.

Immediately the Waps asked, "Why do they wish to kill you?"

John looked at the Waps and thought rapidly. How much should he tell him/it?

Well it knows about Gwen. That alone is unusual.

"They do not like me to have Gwen working here."

"Then why do you do it?"

"To protect her. Another male of our species is trying to kill her."

"Why is that?"

This is getting complicated, John thought.

"This male attacked Gwen in my presence, and I protected her, hurting this male."

By this time another case had arrived, and John proceeded to check it and dispatch it. Gwen helped with the bookkeeping. In between the arrival and dispatch of cases, the question and answer continued.

At some point the men at the other end of the building noticed this, and the supervisor came up and asked, "What's going on?"

"He is asking about Gwen" John replied truthfully. The supervisor gave him a funny look and went back to the end of the conveyor.

In between the arrival and dispatch of the cases the conversation continued. The Waps seemed to be insatiably curious. The presence of Gwen seemed to have stimulated his curiosity.

"Is hurting this male the reason the firm wants to kill you?" Fred asked.

"No, but the male wants to kill me. "

"If this male and the others want to kill you, why are you not now dead?"

"That's logical", John thought, "He must think us completely irrational"

John replied, "The firm wants to keep me alive for the present. I am valuable to them as a trader. When they have a replacement they will kill me."

"When will they have a replacement?"

"In about three month's time. About seventy trading days."

The Waps thought for a moment. "Will your successor trade milk?"

"No. Only I know that you want milk, and I will not tell them."

"Why not?"

"Because if I tell them they will trade milk with you and I will not obtain credit. Then when they want to kill me, and reduce the quality of a consignment to do it, I will not have enough credit to cover the loss."

The Waps thought about this for a moment.

"I understand. For you to live, there must be no-one else who trades milk."

"That is correct. At least for a while. When I have gained enough credit I will cease trading here, take a few gold bars from you, put Gwen on a ship to take her away from here, then go up the line to trade with you all the milk you want."

There was a wait, while the Waps seemed to hum to himself. Or was he communicating with his fellows?

Then the Waps replied, "It seems we are not only gaining milk but your very interesting information from this situation. This is a double advantage to us, worth more than asking another trader for milk. Because of this double advantage, we shall endeavor to keep you alive. We ask in return that you continue to trade milk with us every day. Also when you have placed Gwen on the ship, you return to a place on the line and trade with us large quantities of milk.

"Agreed."

"May I ask you a question?" continued John.

"Yes."

"What is your name?"

The Waps said "My name is …" and there was an un-translated buzzing sound.

"I am sorry that did not translate."

"You are I think the first of your people who asked my name."

"Oh' said John. "May I give you a name?"

"Yes."

"May I call you…..Fred?"

"Yes, that is a suitable identification between us. Fred."

While this was going on they were steadily processing the cases of tea and bags of coffee. Then John noticed that Gwen was looking sad, and avoiding his eyes.

"What's the problem, Gwen?"

"Its all right. Its nothing."

"No, something is troubling you. What is it?"

"Well, this talk of putting me on the ship. I sort of thought I was going to stay with you until you finished here."

"Which will be when they kill me if I stay. Don't worry, they will. The sooner I get out of here the better. And get you on a ship. You won't be safe until then."

She looked troubled, and then looked him in the eye.

"I want to stay with you."

"Gwen! That's not possible. The moment I leave here we will not be protected. We will have to move fast. Those crims will be after us both. I have to get you on a ship fast."

She looked down and asked in a small voice, "Oh. Will I see you again?"

"Of course! When I have gotten rich trading this milk I shall be out of here. We can arrange to meet on another planet."

"Will you?"

"Yes! I really like you. But my first priority is to see you safe."

Gwen smiled and flushed. "Oh, John, I really do like you. I think you are wonderful," she whispered.

The Waps was watching this interchange.

He then asked, "Is this the preliminaries to mating?"

Gwen blushed. John said "No, this is normal conversation between males and females." Gwen blushed even more and looked away.

Chapter Five

For the next two months the trading process continued unabated. John checked, Gwen recorded, and the trade was completed. They increased the deliveries of milk to two liters a day, to the pleasure of the Waps, but that was the limit they could smuggle in their bags without raising comment. John was seriously considering asking for a bar of gold from his Waps friend and cutting and running. It was getting too risky he thought. It was just that the Waps seemed to have an insatiable need for milk, and he hadn't worked out how to cash in the bars of gold quickly so they could get the cash for the tickets to the spaceport. In discussions with Gwen, she was talking about asking her friend at the hotel to cash a gold bar, but as John said, if she could not be trusted they were finished. The amounts he was getting from expenses barely covered the extra the hotel was charging him, plus the food and milk costs. He was in a quandary. He might have risked it, but risking Gwen made things more difficult. "If only I had someone to cash a gold bar for me, maybe two!" he thought.

      "Better hurry up. I have only a month left," he thought. He was caught for the moment.

Then one day, the Waps gave an unusual buzz. "Regrettably John this case contains a product not up to specification. I must deduct the deficiency from your credit."

"Agreed" replied John, "but I checked the case. My machine said it was OK."

"I have noticed that your machines are defective, in that they do not check the quality through to the other side of the case. I have noticed that in these circumstances an inferior quality is placed on the other side of the case," the Waps replied.

"Damn!" said John, "Gwen, get on the other side of the conveyor, and I shall pass you the machine to test that side."

She hopped over, and they double-checked the next case that way. John noticed that the atmosphere of the room had changed. A lot of people were looking up their way with surprised looks.

"We'll see about this," thought John.

The conveyor started again, and a dozen cases later the machine in Gwen's hand gave an angry buzz.

"Defective quality," shouted John, picked up the paint marker and slashed a big red cross on the side of the case, and striking out the code. He pressed the red button, and the conveyor moved backwards, sending cases off the end of the conveyor, which had to be quickly grabbed by the operatives.

"What's this?" came a shout from the other end, "there is nothing wrong with this case!"

John strolled down to the other end, and saw it was Mr Walker. He grabbed the checking machine out of his hand, jumped to the other side of the conveyor and pressed the machine against it. An angry buzz occurred, and the machine flashed red.

"There," said John. "Defective quality. Don't try that again!"

But they did. Twice that afternoon they sent defective cases down the conveyor, twice they were spotted, marked and sent back.

"Look" shouted John, waving his cell phone, "I am going to inform the administration. This is beyond a coincidence."

John had been prepared for this. He moved back behind the green line and rang the court and got through to an official.

"Albrecht and company have tried three times to pass by me cases of defective case of tea. One side packed with an inferior grade."

The official stared at him, while Mr Walker rushed up and began screaming, "Turn that off!" Nobody else tried to cross the green line.

Then an idea occurred to John. He said, "I am upset, and also the Waps trader is very upset." And he waved the phone at the Waps. The Waps said, "Yes, I am upset."

The official gulped "I will send someone straight away!" Mr Walker went pale and ran down to the other end, followed by his men.

"And don't try to destroy the evidence!" John yelled.

Within minutes a vehicle drew up. Mr Walker ran up to him and shouted "Its not my fault. I don't know what he is talking about!"

John walked up and said, "I am the complainant. The other complainant is the Waps trader. He wishes to talk with you."

"Me?"

"You are the officer of the court sent here?"

"Yes."

"Come. The Waps wants to talk to you."

The man very reluctantly went up to the line. The Waps hummed and said, "What John says is correct. Three of the cases had inferior product down one side. It could only be detected on that side by your machine."

The man huffed and said, "This is a serious allegation!"

The Waps replied, "I do not understand. The statement is factually correct."

The court official paled, turned and walked back. "This will be investigated further", he announced.

"What's going to happen?" John asked the court official.

"This will be investigated further," he repeated, turned and headed back to his vehicle.

"Well I am packing it in for the night," John said, picked up his things, said goodbye to Fred, grabbed Gwen's hand and walked out. Fred stood there without a word giving him a strange look.

Mr Walker stood there and said nothing.

"What are we going to do?" asked Gwen as soon as they had put some distance between them and the men.

"We must get a couple of gold bars from Fred. I should have asked for them before I went. I should not have walked out. We are in a pickle. I shall ask Fred for a couple of gold bars tomorrow first thing. Then walk out. Hopefully we can make it to the gold exchange, cash the bars, and then get to the port without being nabbed. We will pick up a couple of liters of milk for Fred." They turned into the supermarket.

When they got out, the found a reception party. "Well" said Rick "You have been handed over to me!" He smiled thinly. "Come on boys!" He turned to his confederates and gestured.

Just at that moment a couple of vehicles drew up and Albrecht security piled out.

"What's going on?" said Rick.

"You can't have him," said a guard.

"What! I was told I could have them."

"The Waps wants them back trading tomorrow morning, unharmed," was the reply.

"Why is the Waps protecting them?" shouted Rick.

"I don't know. I am just following orders. I have to take them back to the hotel, and protect them there. Make sure they turn up tomorrow morning."

With that he gestured towards the vehicle to John and Gwen.

"No thanks, we prefer to walk," said John.

Chapter Six

The next day, there seemed to be quite a crowd at the trading room. Everybody was silent and giving them strange looks. The went up to the line and John said, "This does not look good."

John greeted the Waps "Thank you for saving our lives yesterday."

"How is that?"

"By asking us to be returned here this morning."

"You are valuable to me."

Before he could elaborate, the conveyor belt started up, and Gwen got behind the belt to check the other side.

John noticed that some strange men with hard looks wearing suits were standing behind the green line looking at them. As they were in hearing distance John could not ask the Waps for the two gold bars. But after a while they drifted away and John said, "Fred, I have special request."

"What is that, John?"

"May I have two gold bars from my credit account as soon as possible?"

"May I ask why you want two gold bars?"

"I intend to cease trading and make a run for it."

"I am sorry to hear that, John. Will that mean you will return?"

"Yes, in a few days. I shall appear up the Line, and ask for Fred."

There was a chuckle. "Your request is granted. In a few minutes you will get your gold bars."

During this time they were steadily processing the cases of tea. Then suddenly Fred made a humming sound as if he was communicating with another Waps.

"John, can you stop please. Something has happened."

A case appeared from behind Fred, transported up by another Waps. The top was open. Both John and Gwen looked at it with dread.

"If..if…there is anything wrong I will pay for it."

"John, we agreed on that. But we Waps have a rule. We do not like being deliberately cheated. From our conversation I do not think it was you." And he drew out a device from the case that was filled with sawdust. Fred looked very angry indeed. His wings fluttered and his arms made strange movements.

"Summon me your manager, I think his name is Mr Walker."

John turned and walked up the dead silent row of men, and approached Mr Walker. "The Waps wants to speak to you."

"Why me! If anything has gone wrong it is your fault. That is the rule!"

"Discuss that with the Waps."

A very afraid Mr Walker walked the length of the conveyor, crossed the green line and confronted the Waps.

"Mr Walker," the Waps said, "this device is intended to cheat us." And he held up the device pulled from the chest of sawdust. "It transmits a signal which confuses our checking devices so it appears that the correct quality of tea is in the case. I am very angry."

"If the consignment is defective then it is his fault," screamed Mr Walker, pointing to John, "That is the agreement!"

"Yes, normally," said the Waps gravely, "but in this case John has a substantial credit with us which pays for the loss. As he has no motive to cheat us, I do not believe it was John who tried to cheat us," the Waps continued remorselessly.

"What! What's this credit?" asked Mr Walker in a high-pitched voice, flapping his hands.

John quickly glanced around and stepped back. No one was in listening distance. He looked Gwen in the eyes and shook his head slightly. At the same time Fred produced a red device in his hand.

John and Gwen put their hands on Mr Walker's back and gave him a good shove. He screamed and flapped his hands and fell forward over the line. Fred shot him through the chest with his laser device. Mr Walker fell dead on the floor.

Fred than calmly placed Mr Walker's body on the conveyor and sent it back over the human side. John pressed the red button and the body was carried back to the stunned humans at the end of the conveyor. Not a sound was made.

Then there were stirrings at the end. The men wearing suits rushed to the Line end, their faces contorted and working. Their eyes blazing with anger.

"You!" one man shouted, "You killed him. I saw that. You pushed him over the line!"

"He tried to kill me. He placed that device in the container. It was only just that he was killed. Not me!" John replied.

The man's face became contorted and red. "You are under arrest!" he shouted. He pulled out a badge from his jacket, "FSB. Federal Security Bureau. You are traitors. You have been talking to this….Wasp! I don't know what you have been saying, but I shall find out. I shall extract every last thought from your minds, and then you will go into the gas chamber!" he shouted, waving his arms. The other suited men crowded closer pressing John and Gwen up to the Line.

The Waps began talking. "What John says is correct. He had no motive to cheat me. It was clear his manager knew what was in the chest. As with the agreement someone had to die for the grave default, it should be the person who intended to cheat me. As the manager was clearly one of the guilty ones I chose him to die."

The man in the suit became splenetic. "You keep out of this! It is nothing to do with you! There is something going on between you and I intend to find out!" He made a grab for John.

John was holding Gwen's hand. He turned to look at Gwen in the eye, and they stepped over the line.

The faces of the men facing them went pale and their jaws dropped. They did not make a sound.

A voice behind them said, "Step this way". They turned to see the Waps gesturing to its end of the building. The turned and started walking. Behind them the man started screaming, "Traitors! Waps lovers. You won't get away with this!"

John turned to see him pull something from his jacket. He pushed Gwen sideways suddenly. He felt a beam past his shoulder. It hit a Waps further down the building. Before the man could readjust his aim Fred shot him in the chest with his laser. He then pointed it the other men and said, "Do not do that!"

John got up, helped Gwen up, and hurried her to the other end of the building.

Chapter Seven

The Waps were eying their fallen companion. He was obviously dead, with fluid coming out of his thorax.

They stopped at the entrance and waited. After a short while a Waps whom they recognized as Fred joined them. "More deaths have happened. The matter will now go to higher authority. We will summon a vehicle for you and take you to a safe destination."

Soon a vehicle drew up and a door opened. "You will have to enter and sit. If you have difficulty remember the journey will be short."

They found the seats inside were molded to the Waps anatomy, and hard. But as Fred said the journey was short.

During the journey John noticed that the buildings were much like those on the other side of the line, though the doors were higher. Even the vehicles had a similar streamlined look as the humans', and they even travelled on the same side of the road!

"Plus ca change, plus ca meme chose," thought John, some irrelevant jargon he had picked up somewhere.

They stopped. The doors opened. Fred appeared. He had obviously travelled in front.

"Get out. Follow me," was his brief order.

They followed through a high automatically operating door. They followed Fred down a passageway, the floor covered with some springy material, observed by a number of Waps who stopped dead to look at them, and through another door into a room. There was no other exit.

"Stay here," said Fred. "It may be a long period of time. I do not have sustenance but I can provide liquid."

"Water will do fine," John said. Fred soon reappeared with a carafe of water and two drinking containers and placed them on a table, a bit higher than that used by humans. There were chairs also, obviously useless for humans. The room appeared to a meeting room.

"Plus ca…oh bugger it," thought John.

"You will stay here a long time," Fred said. "If you wish to perform bodily functions, make a sound at the door, and you will be taken to a suitable location." With that he left.

John and Gwen sat down on the floor, occasionally sipping water. At one point Gwen said "I wish to go to the toilet." "So do I," thought John, and got up and knocked on the door. The door opened. "What shall I say?" thought John. "We wish to perform a bodily function," John said to the Waps waiting there.

The translator on his abdomen said "Come", and led them to what was clearly a Waps toilet. There was a hole at the base of a furnishing clearly designed for the base of the Waps body.

"It is a good thing I want to only do a wee," Gwen giggled. Without waiting or asking for John to look away she pulled off her pants, perched on the device, and performed her ablutions. John then urinated on top of it.

"How can we dispose of it?" He poked around. There was a sound and the whole lot disappeared. "I hope we didn't wreck it." The Waps was standing there watching the whole performance, and did not seem too concerned. They then found basins. With a bit of experiment they turned on a flow of water, and washed their hands and faces, but could not find anything to dry themselves. "Better not drink," John said. "We can trust what is in the carafe."

They returned to the room refreshed, and a short time later Fred appeared. "Come," he said.

They were led to another room to face a table presided over by several Waps facing them

Facing the table were two boxes covered with padding. Obviously some attempt had been made to make them comfortable. "Sit," said Fred, and they did. They understood that his shortness was not intended to be discourteous,

Fred took a place on the other side of the table and started without preliminaries, "Your people are demanding your return. Do you wish to return to them?"

"No," said John. He was used to short rejoinders. He nudged Gwen. "No" she said.

There was a short discussion among the Waps at the end of the table.

Fred said, "We have discussed you. You may be valuable to us. For that we have decided to keep you. However there are provisos." At this Fred seemed to chuckle. "First. We need a lot more milk as soon as possible. That is tomorrow. We ask you to go over to your side of the Line, purchase a large quantity of milk, and bring it back over our side."

John was getting used the Waps didactic psychology. "How much?" "We ask for a thousand liters."

John thought. To do that he would have to get back into town to purchase the milk. He would not be able to go to more than two supermarkets before the alarm was raised. Each supermarket would contain first thing in the morning no more than 100 liters…

"I can supply up to 200 hundred liters at one time." He heard Gwen draw a breath. "It is not possible to purchase and transport more without alerting the authorities, and I will be caught."

There was a humming sound among the participants.

"Agreed," said Fred.

The Waps continued. "The next proviso is that you will assist us in setting up another source for this milk."

"Agreed" replied John, "with the understanding that the authorities on the other side of the line will try to terminate this supply, at least temporarily. A continuous large-scale supply will depend on the capabilities of the person chosen to do this, over which I have no control. However I shall do my best to do this."

"Agreed," said Fred.

The Waps continued. "And finally, and most importantly to us, you must continue to supply us with information we request."

"May I ask, do you not have this information from other sources?"

"No, your people are reluctant to supply us with information. It is difficult to talk to your people."

"Why is this?"

"It appears that your authorities consider us a threat."

"Are you?"

There was some discussion about this.

"No. If we are not threatened we will not attack you."

"I will continue to provide information to you, with the proviso that if I consider the information I am asked to provide provides a threat to our people, I will not provide it."

Some humming and the "Agreed." "You may stay on our side of the line".

"I have a request to make," said John.

"What is that?"

"I do not wish to stay with your people for the rest of my life. It is clearly impractical. An additional price is that we return to my people, to our side of the line, within…six months."

More humming at the table. "Agreed, but they will kill you."

"I will have to think of something."

More humming, which went on for a longer period.

"If you are sufficient service to us, we have an alternative proposal to return you to your people with lower risk to you."

"What service?"

"That will be discussed later."

"Agreed," John said. He nudged Gwen. "Agreed," said Gwen.

There was further humming. Then Fred got up and said, "Come."

They followed him back to the room. He said, "Wait here for a few hours. We have no food for you, but I shall fetch more water." He left and returned with another carafe of water.

John said, "We had better get some sleep."

"What is going to happen to us?" Gwen asked.

"I don't know. But relax. Lie down. Try to get some sleep."

The laid down on the floor together. John used his jacket for a pillow, while Gwen snuggled up against him, and used his chest as a pillow. After a moment of his mind wondering he went out like a light.

Chapter Eight

He awakened when he heard the words "John." It was Fred towering above him.

"Don't these creature ever sleep?" he thought.

Both he and Gwen struggled up from the floor.

"You agreed to go across the Line to get us milk," said Fred.

"Yes," said John.

"We have found a place where you can do it. And a person to help you."

"You have? Has he agreed?"

"Not yet. But we think he will. He is one of the friendliest traders. For a great deal of gold I am sure he will help. He has a tent up the line, and trades small quantities of what he calls honey. He is a sole trader. As the quality of this honey is highly variable, he lets us test the quality of this honey beforehand, and is then prepared to negotiate the price afterwards. He does what he calls dicker. As he seems to enjoy doing this, we allow it. He has developed a relationship with our trader. He is called 'Jack' and he calls our trader 'Joe'. Over time we have learned a lot about your people from him. Possibly a lot more than your authorities would allow if they knew."

This was one of the longest conversations John has had with Fred. Mostly the information he had provided had been one way.

"How much gold?" John asked.

"If you say only two hundred liters of milk can be provided, two hundred kilos of gold."

John thought about this for a while. "I don't think that would work."

"Why not?"

"For a start, he will be aware that we are wanted. To tempt him to help us, he needs to see the gold up front, physically. One hundred kilos."

"We cannot pay him unless he provides the milk."

"That's true. But I have over one hundred kilos in my credit account. I will pay for the entire trade. We transport one hundred kilos of gold up to his trading post and put them just short of the line on your side and let him see it. We will tell him that if he assists us and get us back safely that one hundred kilos will be his."

"What about the milk?"

"I was coming to that. We will not tell him that we are getting milk. We will tell him that we need food. In the process of buying food, I will buy all the milk we can find. When I get back and the food and milk has been transferred over the line, I shall inform him of the value of milk. He will understand that if he wants to make a lot more money in a short time he will have to supply you with a lot more milk in a short time. What I know of humans he will do so."

"Why do you not tell him in advance the value of the milk?"

"Because he will cheat us, not you. I will be handed over to the authorities."

"But he will miss out on one hundred kilos of gold."

"He will have the opportunity to make many times that from selling you milk, and be protected from the actions of the authorities."

"I understand. Human behavior is strange. But logical in your own way. I shall order the gold to be delivered."

"Plus an extra bar from my credit account. I need to get cash to make the purchases."

"Agreed."

"I will deliver an unspecified quantity of milk to the line of varying quality. The quality and quantity of the delivery is uncertain. I will do my best to provide you with the maximum amount without endangering Gwen or myself. You will check the quantity and the quality, quantity and quality that I have not agreed in advance. You will then credit my account pro rata, in proportion to the amount delivered, and make your own adjustment for the quality. I will accept your assessment of the value of the quality. Do you agree to this?"

"That is rather a lot, but it sounds logical, I agree to this", the Waps said, actually beginning to sound amused. "But I stress we want a large amount of milk immediately."

"I will get you as much milk as possible. We need to keep you happy. We need to get back over the line."

"Yes, John, you do need to keep us happy," the Waps replied gravely.

It was early morning. They arrived at the tent up the Line on the Waps side, and were introduced to the Waps 'Joe'.

"He will arrive shortly' Joe said. "He usually has several containers of honey."

The Line was in front of them. A carrying device placed the gold in front of the Line.

"Well, this is it," John said, and turned to step over the Line.

"Hey," said Gwen, "you are not going without me!"

"It will be dangerous. Quite possibly fatal," John declared.

"I am coming with you. You need me to pack the shopping baskets. Both of us can do it twice as fast. It will be a lot safer," she asserted.

John agreed. "OK, but we will have to act fast and on the run."

"Speed is my name," she said smiling.

They held hands and stepped across the Line again.

They sat waiting in the tent until Jack turned up. An old van turned up and backed into the end of the tent. A grizzled man with a grey moustache got out and at first did notice them. Then he did and gave a jump.

"Who are you?" he asked.

"My name is John and this is Gwen," John replied.

"What are you doing here?" the man replied suspiciously.

"We need your help", replied John.

"What help?" and then the man started. "Oh, you are the two who crossed the line yesterday. I heard about it. You caused one hell of a stink. I can't help you!"

"Yes, you can," said John. "See that pile of gold over there. It is one hundred kilos. It is yours if you help us this morning. Just a quick trip in your van."

The man eyed the gold. "A hundred kilos. What do you want?"

"Simple. We need food. As you know there is no food for us the other side of the Line. We need to make a shopping trip. Enough food for both of us for a couple of months. A quick trip to a couple of supermarkets to buy enough food. We will shoot in to buy the food, pile it into trolleys and rush out, and pile it into your van. You will be waiting outside in the van. Just a couple of supermarkets. Then we come straight back here, shove the food across the line. No one will see us. You will be quite safe. And you will get your 100 kilos."

The man thought about this for a while, working his mouth and moustache, rolling his eyes and grunting to himself. "That's all?" he said.

"Yes, though we will need some money. You will also need to go into the gold exchange beforehand to cash a gold bar," John replied.

His eyes shone greedily, "A gold bar?" "Yes, but remember if you give us away to the authorities you will miss out on one hundred kilos of gold."

His eyes turned to the pile of gold bars again, and then made up his mind.

"Just help me get these containers of honey out of the van, and across the line," he said. John and Gwen picked them up and just walked them over the line. Jack's faced paled when he saw this.

Then John thought of something. "Oh, and one last thing, if you give us to the authorities, Joe here will not trade with you again."

"I agree," said Joe. Jacks eyes glittered and squinted. "I am not going to give you to the authorities."

"My name is Jack, by the way," he said as they walked to the van.

"I know," John said, "we had better travel in the back," and climbed in to a space smelling of honey. "And don't forget we are going to the gold exchange first. Here is the gold bar."

The doors of the van were slammed shut and Jack climbed into the front. They set out travelling along a bumpy road while Gwen and John sat on the floor and tried to prevent themselves being rolled around. While they could not see outside, they felt it when they arrived onto a smooth road, and heard the traffic noise increase. Then they swung into a parking station, and Jack turned the engine off. Jack turned and said, "Wait here."

John replied, "Now remember what I said. If you give us to the authorities, you will not only lose a hundred kilos of gold but also your trading rights with the Waps."

"Yeah, I heard that," said Jack unhappily.

After he left there was silence in the van. Then Gwen proffered in a small voice, "A ten kilo gold bar is rather a lot of money for a shopping trip."

"I know. But I feel that we will need a lot of cash for later. And Jack is sure to help himself to some of it."

Gwen smiled. "You seem to think of everything," she said.

"I have to stay alive. But it is your life too. If you have any suggestions to make, make them."

"I am quite happy following what you say," she said, laying her head on his shoulder.

After about half an hour, Jack returned and handed him the money. John noticed that Jack had indeed taken a cut out of the wad of hundred Credit notes, but said nothing. "Conditions in the gold market were chaotic. The gold price was not good. You have really caused a commotion," Jack said.

"Lets go and get some food", John said. He was really feeling quite hungry, and his stomach growled.

They went to the supermarket furthest from Jack's tent first. They would visit the other one on the way home.

In the car park, John said to Jack, "Wait here. We are going to go in, grab a couple of trollies, fill them, then push them out here, quickly shove the contents in the back of the van, and take off."

"Do you want me to help?" Jack asked.

"No, you stay in the van. We will need to drive off in a hurry."

Jack seemed happy with that.

While walking through the car park John handed Gwen a wad of cash. She smiled. "All for me?" she said, and stuffed it down the front of her blouse.

"Now listen, Gwen. There will be cameras in the supermarket. The AI will recognize our faces, but it won't be that fast, especially as they won't be expecting us to dive into supermarkets. So we must get in and out fast. Hopefully they won't pick up the van's number in the car park."

"Would they have picked up Jack's face?"

John gave Gwen an appraising glance. "You bet. That is why I kept him out there. They would have chased us back to his tent."

They arrived at the entrance. "Now we don't have time to dawdle. Ten minutes max, in and out. Milk first. We clear the cold cabinet of all milk of any variety, and then all reheating food goes on top. Then we head for the checkout. One each. Hopefully we can get out fast. No stopping for ooops! I need this. No panties. I am sure Jack can be persuaded to do a shop later. Do you understand?"

"Yes, John," was the quiet reply.

"OK, grab a trolley!"

The supermarket was not too full. They went to the milk cabinet first, and cleared it in front of an astounded and indignant lady. Then the food shelves, and piled high the trollies with instant food, clearing the shelves.

"Come on," said John, stopping Gwen wandering her eye to other shelves. "We have six minutes to be clear of here!"

They found at this time of the morning the checkouts were relatively clear. Gwen and John went to separate ones.

John piled the counter high and said to the girl at the checkout "We have a sudden project, and everybody needs to be fed!" She worked through the food and milk methodically. "Bags?" "Yes, please. It will be cash. Yes I will take a receipt."

John packed the trolley, and turned his attention to Gwen, who seemed to have a bit of trouble. "Just pay, while I pack the rest." Gwen seemed inclined to chat, and then colored when she saw John staring intently at her. "No we won't take bonus points, thank you". They rushed the trollies out of the supermarket, and heard faintly sirens a long way away. They charged across the car park, threw open the van door and began throwing in food and drink in higgledy-piggledy. "Start the engine. Climb in!" and the both climbed in the back closing the door as the van took off. They had just made it out the car park as a group of police cars swept by.

"We shall need more food!" John shouted.

"But they are after you!" Jack said.

"We will go to the outermost supermarket. It will be new. Hopefully their AI will not be connected up, or it will take longer to get out there. Now, Gwen, help me stack these packets up or they will be crushed."

At the next supermarket, what was clearly a newly constructed shopping center, they parked again. "Suburbia everywhere," John thought.

"Now Gwen," John said, "you know the drill. This time we need to be even faster!"

"Yes, John," she said meekly.

And they were. If anything could be taken off a record time in and out of a supermarket, this was it. They cleared every milk cabinet, sprinted to the food shelves, and cleared them in a flash, piling them high onto the trollies. They pushed these heavily laden trollies to the checkout, and under the astounded gaze of the manager, they each purchased over a thousand credits' worth of food and milk. This time Gwen kept silent, and avoided the look of the cashier. In fact she slightly beat John. The trip out through the car park was done at a run, and they quickly piled everything in the back.

"We will have to ride in front!" shouted John as he slammed the doors.

This time the police cars did not arrive until they were well down the highway.

"Get down," shouted John, and pushed Gwen down when he sighted them, and they swept past without stopping

"Well, that's it!" said Jack. And it would have been except that John spied a milk bar.

"Stop! I want some more milk. Park up the street from the milk bar."

"Why?"

"I am a milk lover!"

Jack was in an uncaring mood and stopped. John and Gwen leapt out and ran in. There was a big milk cabinet full of milk.

John shouted, "Our people need a lot of milk in a hurry," not untruthfully.

He slammed a hundred credit note on the counter and loaded Gwen's arms with milk, shouting "Come back for more!" as she rushed out. They emptied the cabinet on the second trip, and John shouted "Keep the change," slammed another hundred credit note on the counter and rushed out.

"I think that makes about three hundred liters," said John as they were driving off.

"You certainly like your milk," Jack replied.

"You don't know half of it!" John responded.

Chapter Nine

They returned to the tent safely without being stopped, and quickly unloaded the van, transporting the food and milk directly over to the other side of the Line.

When the transfer was completed, John said "You can have your hundred kilos now." And he picked the bars one by one, stacking then on the other side of the line.

"All yours." "But wait," he continued, "I have something important to tell you."

"What's that?" Jack asked suspiciously.

"See this liter of milk?" and he picked one up to show Jack, "The Waps will pay one kilogram of gold for it."

Jacks eyes widened. "I'll be buggered. Is that true?"

"Yes," responded the Waps Joe behind John, "For the correct quantity and quality we will pay that."

Jack swore and said, "Why didn't you tell me that?"

"Because you would have handed us to the cops. A hundred kilos is nothing to what you can earn now with this knowledge."

Jack looked stunned.

"But a couple of pieces of advice. First you will have to start delivering milk quickly before the word gets around. You will have to clear out all the milk cabinets in the town today and tomorrow, and deliver them here. No later."

Jack moved his mouth and moustache but said nothing.

"The second bit of advice is that you have got to change your normal mode of operations if you want to live."

"What do you mean?"

"You have done this to some extent already with your honey. As the quality of your honey is so variable you could not claim to deliver a particular quality at any time."

"Yeah," said Jack. "A couple of guys who tried that got shot."

"You were forced to deliver the honey to Joe, and rely on his honesty to give you a good price."

"Well, I had to negotiate. Sometimes he offered a too low price!" said Jack.

"No, I have been told the Waps always offered you the correct price from their point of view. They never try to lower the price to make a larger profit. Yes they raised the price sometimes when you dickered. But this was for payment of the information you provided them."

"Information! What information?" cried Jack.

"Apparently when times were slow and you were lonely you struck up a conversation with Joe. He very adeptly questioned you, and you provided him with a great deal of valuable information regarding humans and what happens your side of the line. This information was assessed and valued. You did not know it but you were accumulating a credit amount. When you negotiated a higher amount for your honey you were paid from this credit account."

Jack's eyes widened and said, "I'll be damned."

"Now you see where I am getting at. The Waps psychology is that they will kill you if you do not meet your agreed obligations."

"So? I know that."

"But if you go out, as you surely intend, and deliver so many liters of milk, you will demand so many kilos of gold."

"Yes."

"But you do not know the quality of that milk in those packages. They could vary. Light milk or flavored milk may have a different price from full cream. Under the present system which you intended to use, demanding a kilo for every liter, the Waps will certainly demand your death very rapidly."

Jack paled. "But what am I supposed to do? You have delivered loads of milk of all varieties, full cream, light, and flavored. Yet you are still alive."

"Yes, Jack, but you must listen to me. It is all in the nature of the agreement. You must trust the Waps. You must agree with them that you will deliver an unspecified quantity of milk of an unspecified quality, and rely on them totally to give you the correct price for all you have delivered, whatever the quality, and place it on a credit account, to be drawn on from time to time."

"But won't they try to cheat me?"

"No. Not as far as I know. I don't know how this reputation of cheating Waps came about. But in your case, compared to your life, what if they do screw you down a bit on the price of milk? You will be making millions. And staying alive to spend it!"

"Yeah, I can see your point."

"Joe," John said as he turned to Joe, "You have listened to this. Are you willing to discuss an agreement with Jack in which involves Jack delivering plenty of milk without you killing him? I know milk is important to you."

"Yes, John. I will discuss an agreement with Joe which will avoid him being killed if deliveries are defective."

Later, after Jack had put his gold bars in his van and closed the doors, he sat down with Joe for a chat. He puffed a smoke to relax. It had been a hard day.

Joe said, "Jack, we must change our agreement. I would not like to see you die, and it would also be inconvenient for us."

"Thanks," said Jack.

"You are welcome," said Joe and seemed to chuckle.

"Let us begin. Do you agree to deliver us milk?"

"Agreed."

"Can you agree to a minimum a daily amount?"

"No, all I can do is say I will do my best."

"That is agreed," said Joe. "Can you guarantee a certain quality?"

"No," said Jack, remembering what John said, "There is no way I will be able to know what quality is in each package of milk, and indeed", a thought struck him, "what you define as good quality."

"What would you like us to do?" said Joe.

"I would like you the assess the quality of each packet of milk, and then pay me what you think is fair for that quality and quantity. I shall trust you."

"Agreed," said Joe gravely, bowing slightly. "And how would you like to be paid?"

"I would like you to put the entire amount on a credit account on your side. I will draw it when I need it. In fact that is a good idea. The companies will be after me like bajeezus if I start accumulating a big account at the bank!"

"Agreed."

Jack puffed his smoke.

At that moment two men in suits suddenly appeared at the end of the tent. "Jack MacGearean?" one said. They came up and looked suspiciously at Joe.

"I heard you have a good relationship with your Waps," one stated.

"I am just negotiating the price of my honey. That's allowed."

The man grunted.

"We came earlier. The tent was empty. Where were you?"

"I was out looking for more honey to trade," replied Jack

"People in the neighboring tents said that they heard voices."

"I was talking to the Waps."

The man looked at the Waps, which stood mute.

"Doing what?"

"As I said negotiating. As I said I am allowed! What's this all about?"

The man produced a couple of photographs. "Have you seen these people recently?"

"Like when?" replied Jack.

"Today."

"No," replied Jack.

"Well. There is a reward for them. Ten kilos of gold each."

"Why, what have they done?"

"They have crossed the Line. They crossed into Waps territory yesterday. They have also killed a man. At least one."

"Wellllll.....! If I see them I'll let you know," said Jack.

The men gave the Waps another look, and departed.

Jack sat there smoking, not saying a word. The Waps said nothing either.

Eventually the Waps said, "I wish to remind you Jack that we need more milk."

Jack woke up with a start. "Yes, I had better deposit those gold bars, draw out some cash and clear all the milk cabinets in town."

Chapter Ten

As John and Gwen left the tent, she said, "I wish to go to the toilet."

John looked at the surrounding desert. "Plenty of places round here to do it. I'll come with you."

John said to Fred, "We are going to the toilet, if you don't mind."

Fred replied, "Yes. I shall come with you, if you don't mind."

They walked past the vehicles, into one of which the milk was being loaded, and out into the desert. Gwen found a bush with pink spotted leaves and disappeared behind it. John heard some scratching. John dug a hole in the sand under the grave eyes of Fred.

After they had finished, John asked Fred if they had a supply of water.

"Yes," replied Fred, "I have brought a large container full. I did not know how much you required." He brought this out from his vehicle.

While they were washing, and drinking a few mouthfuls, John heard voices from Jim's tent. He raised a finger to his lips and pointed Gwen to get into the vehicle that had been loaded with their food. The other vehicle had already driven off. She quickly did, and they drove off.

Gwen looked at John and asked, "I have a question for you."

"Go ahead."

"I noticed that you always supplied full cream milk in your trades. What would have happened if one day you had supplied skim milk?"

"I don't know. I was lucky I guess."

She raised her eyebrows looked at him appraisingly, and said, "I'm ravenous! Can we eat something now?"

Fred, who was sitting with them, said, "Yes. Choose packets and you can eat."

They ripped open a couple of packets and scoffed the food.

Fred said suddenly. "As you need perform your bodily functions frequently, I am taking you to a place which has a toilet attached. It is in one of our living units. There you can perform your ablutions frequently, and drink often. We will leave all your food with you."

John asked. "Can we drink the water from your piped water delivery?"

"The water is harmless to you," was the reply.

"Can you also demonstrate how our toilet works?"

"Yes. We have investigated your other emissions. While the devices we have are not built for those products, we have built a device which we hope will work with them."

"Oh, I am sorry for the harm we have caused."

"Your apology is accepted. But your actions were not intentional, and did not cause great harm. In fact we gained from knowledge of your physiology. This gain in knowledge has significantly outweighed the costs."

"I hope we continue to provide you gains which outweigh our costs."

Fred seemed to chuckle. "Yes. We have plans to use you for an important matter in the next couple of days. If the outcome is successful we will repay you a considerable credit amount. We will tell you tomorrow what this matter is."

The apartment, and that what it clearly was, was on the ground floor and faced outside. The windows were opaque. It was furnished, but the furnishings, except for the obvious table, were not built for human use. The bed seemed to be a framework, but only for one, John noticed. The toilet had obviously been built for them. It was their size, sit-down, with a tube going to a large tank beside it. "It works like this", Fred said. He pressed a large flap, obviously built for an exaggerated view of their hands. A vacuum was activated at the hole at the bottom of the device; there was a large roar, which then ceased.

"Very effective," said John, as Gwen clutched his arm. "We shall be careful with it."

"I hope you will be comfortable," Fred said.

"I am sure we will be. Are there light controls?"

Fred demonstrated the usual patches on the wall to activate dimmers.

"We will leave all your food in here. If you want anything open the door, and speak to the one outside. But you cannot leave." With that Fred turned and left.

"Well," said John, "we are in a comfortable enough prison. Lets make ourselves as comfortable as we can."

He picked up a couple of food packages and placed them on the floor to make a pillow, and laid down. After a slight hesitation Gwen got down beside him, put her head on his chest, put one leg across him, and snuggled close.

"Well," thought John, "this is the life!"

When they woke up, it was dark outside. They sat with their back to the wall and discussed what they were going to do next. By this time Gwen was cuddling closely up to him, with her head on his shoulder, looking up at him with an expectant look. She shifted and a leg slid across him. Jim looked down at her face. Her lips opened. A hand came up beside his face. They began to kiss. After much groping and moaning, Gwen pulled off her pants and panties with one hand, opened her legs and gripped him. John quickly pulled off his pants and they made love passionately, one, two, three times.

After they had finished, Gwen said, "I needed that. You could have taken me a long time ago, you know. I loved you from the very start, when you said you were prepared to die for me."

John laughed. "I didn't quite say that. I said I would try to get you on a ship!"

She glanced up, "Do you love me?" and put her hand beside his face.

He looked in her eyes. "Yes, Gwen. I love you. If you are prepared to be my wife, and we get out of this, we shall stick together for the rest of our lives."

She smiled. "What a proposal! Yes I shall stick with you the rest of our lives. In fact, I won't let you out of my sight. I would be bloody stupid to do that, if my past has anything to do with it."

"Your past. Rick and the rest?"

"We won't go into that. I'll tell you one day. But one more time, lover boy!" And she pulled him down on top of her.

They went back to sleep, to be awakened by Fred. "John and Gwen. Have you had a comfortable night?"

"Yes, a very comfortable night."

"I see that you have taken your clothes off. Was the room too hot?"

"No. The room was fine. We sleep like this."

"While you were asleep, a lot has been happening. I wish to discuss it with you."

"Can we perform our ablutions, get dressed and have something to eat, before we discuss it with you?"

"You may."

Which they did, with Fred standing there gravely watching them.

Gwen perked up, saying gaily, "So what's up Fred?"

"I presume you wish me to start?"

"Yes."

"There have been developments over the past day. The humans are extremely angry and have demanded your return."

"Oh, no," said Gwen.

"Do not fear. We will not do that. Not as long as you are useful to us. And you can become even more useful to us."

With that, Fred stopped and waited.

"The humans have demanded discussions. What they call negotiations. To which we have agreed."

Fred continued. "From their transmissions and news broadcasts, which we imperfectly understand, and which we can show you, they feel that in the face of threats from them, we will return you."

"What threats?" asked John.

"Do not be concerned," said the Waps. "Their trade is equally valuable to them as theirs is to us, and they will not interrupt it. Similarly threats of violence and attacks by your ships can be ignored. Our capabilities are far in advance of your peoples', and no sane people will attack us from a position of clear weakness. What I understand of your people, and we have a long way to go in understanding you, these actions are what you call "anger". These actions will not only be irrational, but the opportunity of gain is not there."

John thought, and said. "I feel that your people should be concerned. Even though attempts to disrupt trade, or even violent attacks, are not logical and there is no gain, my people are quite capable of doing this. They can start and continue until the bitter end until all is destroyed. This is how our wars begin. And we have many."

Fred began humming for a considerable length of time, obviously communicating with his people.

"You say that there is a high probability that this will occur."

"Yes. I cannot say what is the likely probability. I would have to read the news and the media reports. The probability is significant. It might be more worth your while to return us than to risk these events." John heard Gwen take an intake of breath.

"However, I have a suggestion which would be beneficial to both sides, and can be very valuable," John continued. He started talking immediately, "I do not know how your trading relations started, but I can see that it is now very inefficient and costly."

Fred replied. "When we began trading, we suffered many defects in the quality of the goods supplied. There seemed to be many disadvantages occurring in this trading. Yet your side ignored our complaints. Only after we raised the level of punishment that we destroyed part of your settlement, that you took notice of us, and instituted this system where the trader pays with his life for any defects."

"Do you do that among your own people?"

"No. If there is a disagreement, the value is assessed, and one side pays the other side. That is logical. We have a fully functioning and logical system."

"So what you have is very much the system I asked for."

"Yes. We were surprised. We originally thought that you were an agent who was placed there to institute gradual change. After what happened it became clear that it was your own idea or initiative.

"How would you like to institute this system now? In all your trading across the line?"

There was a lot more humming.

Then Fred asked, "How can you do that? Are you an agent of your authorities? Is this all an activity to get our attention and cooperation?"

"No. But you have heard of negotiations. Dicker as Jack calls it. If you produce me, I can face the authorities and negotiate a change."

There was more humming. "We intended that you talked to your people. We were hoping if you spoke to them, you would reduce their demands and explain that the death of Mr Walker was just and necessary. For that service, for what you have already done for us, and more information on your people, we would have returned you to your side in a situation where there was no harm to yourself. But if you could change the trading system to what we prefer, that would be very valuable for us. You would gain a lot of credit. We would certainly return you to your side, and after the costs of doing it, you may have still a lot of credit."

"Thank you Fred. Bring those media reports to me, and we shall have a discussion of the tactics we shall take. Oh, and one last thing. If we are going to stay here more than a few days we would like what we call a shower set up."

"What is that?"

"It is device to wash our entire bodies. We cool our bodies by exuding a salty liquid that evaporates. The salt and organic residues remain on our skins. This begins to feel uncomfortable unless they are washed off. We like to immerse ourselves under a spray of water to wash off these solids. What is needed is a spray device fixed to the ceiling and a piped supply of water. There must be controls to operate the spray and the temperature of the water. Also there must be a hole in a sloped floor for the water to run out of the room. We also require what are called towels, one for each of us, which is thick material about our size that we use to dry ourselves. Further complication such as fans to remove damp and doors to limit splashing may be added later. Do you think you can manage this? I do not know your familiarity in the use of water. You may deduct the cost of this expensive facility from our credit."

"We will do our best," said Fred.

Chapter Eleven

"Can you read the writing on these reports?" John asked, looking up at the Waps from the reader.

"Yes, our original negotiations with your people included lessons on how to read your writing, and indeed how to speak you language. Good relations have since become less easy, but at one time we met a number of humans who were like you, willing to be cooperative. We in turn gave them information on how to read our writing and how to speak our language. From these translators were developed."

"I presume a number of these readers have been purchased," said John.

"A few. It has become more difficult to purchase these and other items."

"Thank you for that information. Now these readers receive transmissions from the other side of the line. Whether or not the humans are aware of this, they have not thought it important to block these transmissions. I do not know how things operate on this side of the line, and I am not asking. You must assess the value of the information I provide, and credit me the usual way."

"As you can see," John continued, "I can change what I see on the reader by a number of ways, including touching this switch. This is the basic news switch. It accesses many different news sources. All of them report news, events which are currently happening. They also report comments and opinions on this news. The news reports, even on the same event, also vary in the way they are written. These differences are caused by the 'bias' of the individual channels. We humans do not necessarily consider that bias is bad, because we tend to read only those media channels that we agree with overall. This bias may match our overall opinions and wishes. The average human can only read two or three of these news channels at the most. We can also view moving pictures and verbal statements on these readers. Do you understand me so far?"

"Yes."

"The news sources, which we call 'channels', are normally free to the viewers. They make money to support themselves from advertising, which are invitations to buy products, or they are owned or subsidized by firms that pay them money. However in that case the people who pay them money usually have a direct say in what is transmitted. Do you follow me? This is important."

"Yes." the Waps said.

"What I see is that there is currently almost universal anger and hysteria in the media, on nearly all the channels. Our crossing the line has upset very many people, from the top to bottom of our society. They are not being cool and logical about this. While the two deaths have certainly made things worse; while I am called a 'murderer' or killer, which your people are accused of protecting, a more fundamental issue seems to have been triggered, as the most angry and hysterical sources of news I know are owned by and subsidized by the major trading firms. Why is this I do not know at present. I will have to think about it. Maybe there is something I don't know. If you are willing to supply me with this knowledge for free, it will help me provide you with better advice."

There was a humming sound. "I will consult. I will return in a short time."

After the Waps left, Gwen spoke up. "What do you mean? Charging you for information?"

"Gwen, I think I have worked out a basic part of the Waps personality, and you must realize that they do not think like humans."

"I know they don't think like humans," Gwen replied.

"Wait! ….I know they are not human. But I do not think many people have realized that their psychology is fundamentally different. I realized subconsciously when I started to work with Fred. Basically when you are dealing with a Waps, a Waps will charge you for everything. You are constantly running up a credit or debit balance with them. They are fundamentally moral when they do this. They do not overcharge or cheat you. It seems that they are genetically incapable of doing this. Maybe it part of some sort of hive mentality. But if I asked them for some information, they would charge me for it. As I am unaware of the value of that information to them I am very careful not to ask them anything, though I am dying of curiosity. We have run up a large credit balance with them, but I hate to think what would happen if that credit balance runs out!"

"Oh. What a scary thought." Gwen shuddered.

"So be careful what you say. I am very pleased you keep your mouth shut. Continue to do so if you can."

"That's not hard. I'm scared of them!" Gwen answered.

"No, just regard them as coldly logical. I am sure that they are charging us for this accommodation, and every drop of water we drink. But don't worry. I am sure it is not excessive. Our credit should last a long time, and I shall try my best to run it up further."

"Oh dear!" Gwen replied, and then looked troubled, and she continued. "But I have noticed you tend to think like the Waps. Even from the start. Though I love you madly, there seems to be something cold about you deep down. Until last night you showed no passion, though you have had plenty of opportunity!" She giggled and put her hand on his chest, looking into his eyes.

John thought for a little while. "Gwen, I do love you madly, though sometimes I won't display it. If we stick together, remember regardless of what I do or say, or my apparent coldness, I love you like crazy. Remember that always." He looked in her eyes, and his eyes watered.

"Oh, John! What is it?" she cried.

John sighed. "I have been tested as a psychotic. That does not mean I am one of those axe-murder people. I am just devoid of normal feelings. It is not that I am incapable of loving you. It is just that from what I understand I am incapable of showing those feeling normal people have. I am always calculating, calculating. Just like the Waps, I suppose."

"Oh, John, how terrible!" Gwen hid her face in her hands and sobbed.

"Gwen, I do love you. Regardless of what happens I will do my best to get you back to a human society. And when I get you there, you won't owe me anything."

"Oh, John," she cried, grabbing him in her arms, "I will stay with you always. I love you! I will never leave you! Not for anything." She buried her head in his chest and began to cry. John held on to her and stroked her back.

At that point Fred returned. "Is this another preliminary to sexual intercourse, and shall I leave?"

"No, we are having a discussion. Sometimes discussion between human male and females take this form. And what is the result of your discussions?"

"We have decided to discuss the matter with you, free of charge. It happened about a hundred years ago shortly after the first negotiations began between our people."

"Yes. What happened?"

"We killed your diplomats."

"You did what?" said John. Gwen interjected, "Oh my gawd!"

"You're crazy," said John. "That would have led to instant attack by our battlefleet!"

"Yes, that happened," replied Fred.

"But why? I know you are not mad. You are supremely rational. But it makes me feel ill and want to back away from you!"

"We were not aware that this would be the reaction," the Waps said.

"It is the same from the point of your feelings of somebody going through your young and eggs with a laser. You just don't do that!"

"I understand. But why?"

"I suppose because we have so many wars. It is understood that diplomats are there to prevent and cease them."

"Yes. We made a serous mistake. It has led to many years of dislike and suspicion."

"Why did you do it?" John asked.

"After the original discussions and commercial exchanges, it was agreed to swap negotiators who would proceed to our respective home planets to continue discussions and find out more about each other."

The Waps waited, and continued. "We exchanged twelve members of each other's species and as agreed carried the humans to our home planet. It was a major cost, but it was compensated by the similar costs incurred by your own people taking our people to your home planet."

"Then?"

"Your humans were lodged in what they agreed was comfortable accommodation in our main city. The only requirement which we stipulated was that they did not travel unaccompanied and communicated their wishes with us always."

"And?"

"A female of your species managed to evade our supervision – and entered a nursery, I suppose you would call it, to view our young. She was not immediately seen, as none of our people would even think of entering unless for the purpose of leaving their young to be reared. She picked up one of the young. She was seen. For reasons that I will not discuss, she was killed. She was actually ripped to pieces by the staff of carers. There was a furor, as you call it. The guards were executed for their negligence. Before the guards' execution, it became clear that the humans had co-operated among themselves to distract the guards so this person could slip away, and had knowledge of her intended activity. Under our law and processes, cooperation in the commission of a capital crime means death. They were executed."

"We informed your government, and even returned the bodies, and tried to explain the reason for the executions. The reaction was as you describe. We have been hated by your species ever since. Our diplomats were returned to us unharmed several years later."

"I see," said John. "I can see that the fault was partly ours. Maybe the entire team were not diplomats. We could have included scientists to study you. As our scientists are very curious, they might play tricks to get round your prohibitions and get more information. They did not fully understand you and your reactions."

"That is true. But since then no human will cross the line to talk to us. The only talk to us from the other side of the line."

"But don't you kill people who cross the line?"

"Yes, that is the agreement we have since made. Your people have said that you will kill any of our people who cross the line. And you do."

"Then why didn't you kill us?"

"For two reasons. First, it was clear that your own people wanted to kill you. Second, we expected to gain from having you on our side of the line. We needed a large quantity of milk, which you could supply immediately, and we discerned that you were somewhat different from your people, more friendlily to us, and we could talk logically to you. We also saw that you would not help us if we harmed Gwen, and as she is a female we are further constrained from harming her."

"I won't ask you why you need the milk," said John.

"I am allowed to inform you of that important information on the condition that you do not inform your own people."

John thought of that. "Will this information constrain our return to our own people?"

"Yes it will have that effect. It will certainly reduce your credit."

"No, I do not want this information, unless it is vital for my forthcoming duties, when you must provide the information free, and it must not constrain our return to our people."

The Waps seemed to think about this. "We will consider this matter.

John started talking. "Now we must discuss the reaction of our people. They are clearly very angry. If you do not understand that term, regard it as an instinctive emotional reaction in response to hurt. The response is usually violence, unless kept in check by legal and society sanctions. The way to reduce anger is either through the passage of time, or through reason. Or both. By passage of time I mean you have to wait a long time before again approaching the angry person. If you cannot do that, through reason means approaching the angry person in a situation where he is prevented from attacking you, and discussing the situation. Often, but not always, this reduces anger. They cease wanting to attack you."

"I think I understand you so far", said the Waps.

"Anger can also be felt by a group of humans, or indeed all human society at the same time. That can be a very dangerous situation."

"I can see that," said the Waps.

"But humans have evolved a system of discussing these things. Representatives of the angry groups can be appointed, and can meet together without attacking each other. The cause of the anger can be discussed. If their disagreements are resolved their anger is reduced, and they then usually produce an agreement which covers their behavior for similar situations in the future."

"I understand. But how does this help us in this present situation?" asked Fred.

"The humans are instinctively expecting that you ask for a meeting between the two species. You can say that you will produce the two of us, and meet in a suitable location on the Line, facing each other on each side of the line. They will agree to this request. Their primary demand will be for our return, but there will be an unspoken agreement that there will be discussions on the current differences, and this is important, any agreement made at this meeting will be binding on both species. For this they will send their senior representatives. "

"How will this meeting be conducted?" asked the Waps.

"That is uncertain, at first. Probably many will be present at the beginning. The unspoken agreement will be that, if you do not immediately hand us over, I hope, the meeting will be conducted over many days and what will be their underlying concerns will be discussed. In the end the agreement will be made by a few."

"They will not immediately make the demands which most interest them?"

"No, do not expect rationality. They need to do what we call vent their anger. It is also a human habit in these negotiations to hide their true intentions at first. This is what they call the negotiation process."

"That is strange and wasteful of time and effort!"

"That is true. But humans no doubt regard you as strange too. You probably concede important things first, and then become totally recalcitrant. This must frustrate the negotiators."

"Yes. This has appeared to have happened."

"So I suggest that you request a meeting. You say that you will produce the two of us on your side of the line. But you must promise me not to hand us over under any circumstances. With your permission I will lead the negotiations over several days, and hopefully this will lead to a mutually satisfactory agreement for both sides."

"Yes. We will not hand you over. If you can do what you say we will be very pleased."

"Good. Then you must tell me free of charge for the purpose of these negotiations what your people mainly want. I will do my best to secure this outcome for you."

There was further humming from the Waps. "That is not a great secret. We have made our desires known to the humans for many years. First, we find this method of trading unsatisfactory. We much prefer the method that we agreed with you. If there is a dispute over quality or quantity, this matter is settled by an adjustment to our mutual credit balance. Second, this prohibition on our peoples' travelling among your people on the pain of death must be lifted. We would like to view your society, and how it works. Third, we find the level of armed confrontation illogical. There is no real need for it. We do not consider ourselves a threat to you. You certainly cannot be a threat to us.

"I will do my best for you, at least as far as number one is concerned. Number two and three are more problematic, and will take many years of gradual adjustment. It is doubtful that these discussions will solve those problems. But probably more normal trading rules will eventually allow number two, and then three. There will be several meetings, and the people will be very noisy. Gwen and I will walk out of at least two of them. After that they will calm down, and calm discussions will begin. They will forget their desire to have us returned when they realize that can make gains in the trading agreement. You will leave these discussions to me. Is that agreed?"

There was a humming sound. "Agreed."

Chapter Twelve

The human side of the room was crowded. It was a large room that covered the Line, a white line engraved on the floor. It was the Court Room at the equator. On each side there was a Judge's chair facing the other. There were also benches and seats in front of the judges' chairs. On the human side these were railed off from the chairs for the onlookers. Directly in front of the judges were the docks for the accused. On the human side glass panels enclosed it, no doubt to prevent the accused trying to escape.

There was wild commotion in the room, which intensified when John and Gwen walked into the room. There were two seats for them, padded boxes the right size, this time with backs to lean on. They took their seats.

The human judge, dressed in a gown, called for order, and there were continuous calls by official members of the court until some semblance of quiet was achieved.

"I call the court to order!" shouted the human judge.

Before the sound died down, John said. "This is not a court, and I am not on trial!"

There was immediate bedlam. A man wearing a gown in the front row jumped up and shouted, "That is what you say! You are accused of murder! You killed a man by pushing him over the Line and having him shot by a Wasp! We have witnesses."

"The Waps desired to kill him for cheating them. His execution was part of the Agreement. He deliberately supplied a case of defective quality."

"That's what you say!" shouted the man. The room erupted into a storm of name calling including "Traitor!" and "Waps lover!".

John stood up and said, "Mr Chairman, if you do not restore order on your side, I shall terminate this meeting."

The judge/chairman went pale. "You can't do that! I call on my Waps judge colleague to hand these humans over to us immediately."

The Waps gravely replied, "I will not do that. What the human said is the truth. The man Mr Walker deliberately tried to deceive us by installing a device in the case to deceive our detectors. John clearly was unaware that this had happened. Under the agreement the human responsible had to die."

"How do you know he was unaware?"

"We were watching him. He and his female assistant each used their detection device on the case on opposite sides, and the device showed that the correct quality was in the case. Our device was deceived as well. We found the deliberate fraud when we opened the case, and found a transmitting device inside it. We can show you what happened by transmitting a three dimensional image of the event, if you wish."

The judge rolled his eyes, looked sideways and said "That will not be necessary. We will not accept your images as evidence anyway. But we insist that you hand over the humans!"

"No," replied the Waps. "I may also point out that that one of your people killed one of our people."

"That was an unfortunate accident. One of your people killed one of our people."

John said, "That was not an accident. Your man shot at me, in Waps territory, narrowly missing me!"

"Silence!" yelled the judge. "You are not allowed to speak unless questioned!"

John smiled grimly. "This is not a trial. It is a meeting. As you are unable to control this meeting, this meeting will cease. It will meet tomorrow at the same time, but only on the condition that, first there is no shouting and abuse, and second I am not having the following in the room." And he pointed to the prosecuting counsel, his assistants, and then for good measure a number in front rows of the audience who were giving him particularly dirty looks. They went bright red and rose from their chairs.

There was again uproar. The judge shouted "Order! Order! I am not having that! You will stay!"

"I may point out that you are being broadcast. Your paymasters will not be happy how things have gone. I suggest that if you cannot control this meeting, and can't be chairman, they can find somebody else!" With that he took Gwen's hand, stood up and began to walk out.

"Wait!" shouted the judge. One of the lawyers in the front row shouted "Traitor. You have been trading with the Waps! Milk!"

John turned and asked, "How did you learn that?"

"Because we have questioned your confederate. He has admitted supplying milk at your behest!"

John said, "So Jack is in your custody."

"Yes he is! He has admitted everything, including your foray to our side!"

John said grimly, "I want Jack to be in this room tomorrow, sitting on the front row, together with his lawyer. If he is not here we will not return," pointing at the judge.

With that he turned and left, followed by Gwen. The Waps calmly stood up and walked out. Yelling and the consternation of the human crowd followed their exit.

"They have contacted us and attempted to persuade us to return you," said Fred next day.

"And the result?" asked John.

"We have refused. The meeting yesterday was most informative. We have gained a lot of information on the psychology of humans. Is this an exhibition of anger?"

"Yes," replied John, "sometimes it gets worse. Maybe today will be another exhibition of anger for your information. But I am getting there. In a few days they will be beginning to see sense, as the humans say. Do not be concerned. There are powerful influences working behind the scenes. When they see that that you will not return us, they will turn their attention to those other issues. I will negotiate for you and try to get what you want, at least for your first request on trading."

"Agreed. This is a very interesting process," said Fred.

When they entered the room next day, the crowd was a lot quieter. John noted that Jack was sitting near the end of the first row, his face very bruised.

"Mr Chairman," said John. The judge paled, and looked uncomfortable. "I have asked the Waps to check to see that every person I pointed out yesterday is not in the room. A number are in the room, in the rear rows. This meeting, this meeting, will not commence until they have all left."

John turned to Fred. "Which are they?"

There was humming. "The person you called the prosecuting counsel is in the rear row, third seat along. His friends, two of them are next to him. Other persons you pointed at are also in the room, five in all, in rows further in. If the human chairman allows me, I will point a non-harmful laser at these persons. They will then leave."

"I will not allow you to do this!" the Chairman shouted.

Immediately John and Gwen turned to leave. Simultaneously all the other Waps rose.

"Wait!" the Chairman turn around yelled. "Will all those who were asked to go, go please!" There was mumblings and stirrings and a number of people left.

"Is that all, Fred?" John asked. "No two have remained. On the third row, second in, and fourth row, next to the end." There was silence. The Chairman turned and looked. "I am sure these persons were not among those pointed out yesterday!" He tried to sound confident.

"I am sure they are!" said John.

"This is most irregular," said the Chairman. There was a wait, and two men got up and left.

There was an angry mumble.

"Mr Chairman…." began John.

There was a sudden shout. "Bastard!"

Everybody turned to look. A man stood up. It was Rick. "You are not going to get away with this! Traitor! Waps lover!" With that he pulled out a gun and aimed it at John and Gwen. Without thinking John pushed Gwen down, knocking down Fred, and jumped on top of them. There was a zap of red flame that burned the seats behind them.

Immediately there was a Waps voice "Stop! Or you all die!"

There was silence. Then three or four men jumped on the yelling Rick, pulling the gun from his hand.

When the furor died down, John said, "Place the man in the dock!" Rick screamed and struggled. He knew what was coming. He was placed in the dock and the glass door closed.

"Were there any Waps injuries?" asked John.

Fortunately there were none, though here was loud humming among the Waps.

By this time Rick's yells were reduced to whimpering, and he cringed in the dock.

John asked Fred. "What are the rules of agreement in a case like this?"

"He clearly shot into Waps territory with the intent to kill. The agreement is clear. He dies, or we take punitive action," the presiding Waps replied.

"No! No!" shouted Rick. "I did not kill anyone! I missed!" He fell to his knees and began crying.

A thought occurred to John. Maybe this would short cut these interminable negotiations.

The court, as that was what it had become, was quiet as they all stared at the human in the dock.

"Does the sentence have to be carried out immediately?" John asked.

"No," said Fred, "but we do not like inconvenient delay."

"Would you mind this matter to be dealt with another way?" asked John.

"Is there a reason?" asked Fred.

"Two reasons. An execution will terminate our negotiations for a while. Secondly I think that in return for handing this person over for trial in a human court, we may be able to obtain an agreement to commence negotiations on the matters we discussed."

"Will the human court kill him?" Fred asked.

"Not necessarily. As no one was killed, our laws may give him a lighter sentence. If you are willing to overlook the shooting into Waps territory." Rick began to look hopeful.

There was a buzzing sound. "Agreed."

John turned to the judge. "You heard that. In return for handing this man over to your courts on the charge of attempted murder, shooting into Waps territory, and risking the lives of everyone in this town; in return, I want an agreement that this so called court will re-convene as a meeting tomorrow to negotiate some pressing matters which the Waps want discussed. And these discussions will proceed sensibly and calmly."

The judge looked left and right, and there was a hurried conference. "We agree."

"Furthermore," said John, "I want Jack released immediately and returned to his trading post, and every day he is supplied with a thousand liters of milk to supply to the Waps. This milk supply has priority over any other milk supply. And I do not need to point out the consequences of any attempt to contaminate or reduce the quality of this milk. As our forthcoming agreement will show, you, not Jack will pay the penalty." Jack looked dumbfounded; his mustache quivered, and began to show signs of hope.

"And finally, I want a new chairman for this meeting. Not you!" and he pointed at the judge. "This whole affair has been handled ineptly and incompetently. You are clearly incapable of controlling this meeting or its participants!" The judge paled.

And with that, John and Gwen walked out.

Chapter Thirteen

After they left, Fred led John and Gwen to a group of Waps standing in a semi-circle. "What has been achieved today?" asked Fred.

"The humans are now no longer angry. They are what we call chastened. They have been returned to a calm and rational frame of mind. That is an important step. They will now be willing to discuss and negotiate. Their demands to have us returned will not be raised again unless they do not gain from the negotiations. Also another gain is that while negotiations continue they will allow Jack to supply 1000 liters of milk a day. If they are happy with the outcome of the negotiations, this milk supply will continue, and they will probably be willing to supply more."

"Those are very satisfactory outcomes. We are very pleased," replied one of the Waps.

"Now for the negotiations to succeed, you must allow me to conduct them. Only I know what the human psychology is. If I am the chief negotiator, you must clearly inform me beforehand of what you want, with their given priorities, and also what you are willing to give in exchange, and how much. I will discuss every step I take with you as we go, and the negotiations will be slow. The humans expect this, and expect the negotiations to continue over many days. You will have the right to stop me at any point, if I say something you do not like, or indeed refuse to accept any agreement I make. I shall be very careful in what I say. Do you agree to this?"

There was a lot of discussion among the Waps in the semi-circle.

"The question we raise is the question of trust. Even if we are there listening how do we know that you are negotiating for our interests over the long term?"

"That is a problem. I cannot answer that. I suggest that you allow me to negotiate the bare minimum only, which are the trading protocols, and no other matter. That way you minimize your risk," replied John.

"That is logical," said the Waps. There was further discussion. "We will allow you to conduct the negotiations on our behalf. Shall we now tell you what we want?"

"Yes," said John.

"We want the trading system changed. Instead of the present system we want the system to work using mutual credit balances. Each side checks the quality and quantity and adjusts the credit balance. If there is a dispute it must be decided in some logical manner," the chief Waps said.

John thought a short while, and then suggested, "We have a system called arbitration. If there is a commercial dispute it goes to persons called arbitrators, who settle the matter. Their decision is final."

"Does this system work?" asked the Waps.

"Yes, it works most of the time. To be employed as an arbitrator, this person has to gain a reputation of honesty, which they are reluctant to lose," said John. He continued, "You could have two arbitrators deciding at the same time, one of your people and one of ours. This will reduce the chance of a breakdown in the arbitration system. No one will want this, and the arbitrators will take great care to see that this does not happen."

There was further humming. "We like that proposal."

"However to make a proposal you must make a concession in return."

"Concession? Our proposal is logical and beneficial to all," relied the Waps. If he could sound surprised he would be.

"I agree. But humans do not think like that. You must first offer the humans what they find beneficial, and want," John replied.

"What would that be?" asked the Waps.

"The humans find the system of executing traders abhorrent. They do not like it. Furthermore it imposes large costs on the trading firms, as they have to pay people a large amount of money to people to risk being traders," John replied. "You could offer a change in the agreement that no-one is killed."

"But that is a logical part of our agreement!" the Waps replied, "If we adjust the credit no-one gets killed."

"Ah! But you must make the proposal to appeal to human psychology first. Their feelings.

Put it to them as a concession. That way they will be more willing to accept your proposal."

There was further discussion among the group. "Are you saying the way we put the proposal increases the chance of it being accepted?" the Waps asked.

"Exactly!"

"We find that very strange. We are glad we are employing you as our negotiator." All the Waps hummed in agreement.

"Is that all you want in the negotiations?" John asked.

"That is essentially what we want. We can discuss this matter more tomorrow after we have had an extensive discussion."

"There is one more thing. Please can you give Jack a shopping list from us? There are many things he could get us from the other side which will add to our comfort."

" A list of things to buy? Yes, we can do that."

"We will pay him a kilo of gold to buy these things for us. If you supply us with a writing instrument, we can use the wrapping paper from our supplies to write the list on. You can supply this list and our instructions to Jack."

"We will do that."

Back at the apartment John asked Gwen, "What do you need?"

"Toilet paper, panties,…give me the list! John. I will write it. Lets see…soap. Hmmm…."

The next day was commenced with another discussion with the Waps.

"I have thought what our strategy should be. I think it would be best if we make all three demands at once – the change in the trading agreement, second the opportunity for the Waps to cross the Line on this planet and travel to other planets, and third the reduction in armed confrontation. "

"Why should we make all these demands at once?" asked Fred.

"Because if you make just one demand they will automatically refuse it. If you make three, they will reject two, and accept one if you make it worth their while. That is human nature," said John.

"That is illogical. All requests should be considered on their merits," said Fred.

"'Fraid not. That's not how it works with humans," replied John.

There was further humming among the watching Waps.

"And another thing," said John. "We must at the very start ask how they intend to try this man who shot at us. This will prevent them getting angry, and raise fear among them. They will be relieved when the negotiations start. Otherwise they may get belligerent, and delay negotiations."

There was further humming. "If this is correct, we are glad you are conducting our negotiations."

"And Gwen," John said turning to Gwen, "You have to sit there and say nothing. You will find it very boring. If you feel the need to say anything, just whisper to me. Otherwise sit there and look wise. But it is necessary for you to be there. If the negotiators try to draw you in, say something short and non-committal only. For you silence is golden." Gwen laughed.

"Is everyone prepared? Let's go in."

Chapter Fourteen

The humans were ready and waiting for them. The personnel facing them had completely changed. A table had been installed, and a number of rows of seats had been removed. There were also far fewer people in the room. A line of humans sat at the table facing them.

The Waps had left their furniture unchanged, including the seats for the humans, though they had replaced the burnt coverings on the backs. John and Gwen sat down.

John looked at the reader he carried, which he had adapted to make notes.

"Mr Chairman," he said, addressing the man at the center of the table, a thin dark man quite different from the somewhat chubby judge with whom he had previously contested, "I first need to ask what arrangements have been made for the trial of the man who shot at us. You may remember that this unusual concession of a human trial for a man who shot into Waps territory and nearly injured or killed a number of Waps was allowed on the condition that these negotiations take place calmly and with the purpose of reaching a settlement. If you fail to adhere to that conduct the Waps have the right to ask for the man to be returned to this court for a summary trial."

One of the onlookers stirred. John noticed it was the father of Rick.

"These negotiations…" He stopped. The man behind him stirred. "Will be conducted diligently and calmly as the Waps requested." He looked at John with new respect in his eyes. "The man who shot at you is being held in custody, and has been charged with attempted murder. He will be brought to trial in the near future."

"Very well. Let the negotiations begin. The Waps have asked me to conduct these negotiations on their behalf, under their constant supervision. From time to time we will stop and confer. If there is any misunderstanding regarding what I have said, I will clarify," and here John smiled, "what I have previously said. Both sides will record what we have said and indeed what we eventually agree. Eventually the new agreement will be placed in writing in both the human language and the Waps language. I need hardly remind you that the Waps can read our language. Is that understood?"

There were murmurings between both sides. "Mr Chairman. Is that understood and agreed?"

"Yes," said the Chairman.

"Now, Mr Chairman," said John, smiling, "I need to extract a minor concession from you."

"What's that," the Chairman asked suspiciously.

"As you are aware, the Waps language is highly logical. As you are also aware that as a consequence, all agreements with the Waps so far have used the Waps language version as the authoritative text. If we eventually manage to reach a written agreement, I would like this tradition continued and the Waps version of the agreement to be the authoritative text."

There was silence. The Chairman looked at the other men at the table. They huddled together and began to discuss, referring to references.

Finally the Chairman turned back. "We agree. But don't think we will be happy to make so many other concessions so easily."

There was humming among the Waps in the background, but no interruption.

John smiled. "I am sure that you will find this agreement highly profitable and necessary. Both sides have lost through what are only misunderstandings."

"Now," continued John, "in summary, and the details can be worked out later, the Waps desire three main changes in Waps-human relationships and ways of doing business."

"First, the Waps find the present method of doing business unprofitable and inconvenient, and wish to change it."

"Second, the Waps wish to cross the Line, and travel safely among your people."

"YOUR people....!" the Chairman interjected.

"Stay calm," John said, "They wish to travel safely on the surface of this planet, to trade and other things, and also to travel to other human planets." There were laughs along the table.

"And the third demand?" asked the Chairman.

"Request," said John, again smiling. "The Waps find this armed confrontation wasteful and unnecessary, and wish to reach a mutual agreement to reduce it."

"What?" said the Chairman, barely controlling himself.

Somebody else on the table said, "How do they propose to do this?"

"This is a matter of further negotiations, conducted with trust and good faith," replied John sweetly.

"No, way!" they virtually all shouted.

"All these matters are up for discussion. However on the first issue the Waps are willing to concede that no-one gets executed if there is a dispute over quality."

There was silence, and they stared at him. "How will this work?" asked the Chairman.

"By arbitration," said John. "Let me explain. In Waps society, very much as in human society, trade is carried out between Waps using mutual credit accounts, not the cash on the nail basis, which is conducted on the Line at present. Credit accounts can be drawn on when requested."

"I seek confirmation from my Waps colleagues on this," John turned to Fred. There was humming. Then Fred said, "That is largely true, John. While we use what you call cash for small transactions, trading is conducted by mutual credit accounts. These accounts are maintained by an institutional structure."

"See? Despite appearances the Waps are very similar to us. Yes, and from time to time the

Waps have disputes over quality and quantity. Under this situation, so the Waps inform me, they resort to an arbitrator, who settles the dispute. The credit account is then adjusted on the instructions of the arbitrator. Very calm and logical. No one gets killed."

John turned to Fred. "I require you to confirm what I said was correct."

After a bit of humming, Fred answered. "What John said is correct in operation, making minor allowances for the language. We do trade with credit accounts, we do from time to time have disputes over the quality and quantity of the delivered good or service, and these disputes are settled by what you call an arbitrator in a fast and efficient manner. And yes, no one gets killed." Fred seemed to hum in amusement.

There was silence.

John said, "I see that you have a lot to take in. I suggest that we all take a break, and we return at the second hour this afternoon. And before we go, I need hardly remind the major trading firms, and he smiled at the hidden cameras, "the major savings in salaries if no-one is killed in a trading dispute from now on."

They all left the room.

"That alone will force them to talk turkey when they return. Maybe I can even get them to allow short term visitors to the other side, if I can couch it in terms of highly placed buyers visiting the major trading firms." He felt very smug and proud of himself.

Fred asked after they had left, "What is your assessment of the success so far?"

"To use a human term, when they return they will be eating out of my hands. Except for the details they will be willing to concede point one. If they are sufficiently pleased they may be willing to concede part of point two, and allow selected Waps to travel to appointments on the human side."

There was buzzing among the Waps. "We are very happy if this happens."

"There is a lot more work to do. As we humans say, the devil is in the detail. This will take several days before we get a written agreement. If you will allow me, I will continue the major negotiations on point one, and initiate an agreement on point two. Then I can hand over detailed negotiations to your people, with me sitting next to you to provide advice."

"And point three, the armed confrontation?"

"If things go very well, I can ask them if they will be willing to consider this issue. If they are agreeable, I can suggest separate negotiations be commenced. This is a very delicate matter and you would be right excluding me from the negotiations. It will also take a long time. I would be happy to continue to provide advice, but I must remind you that you promised me that you would return me to my own side without risk to me if I provide you with a sufficiently valuable service."

"That is true," said Fred, "but it goes beyond mere logic to say that we will be sorry to lose you."

Chapter Fifteen

Back at the apartment the Waps were installing a shower.

Fred asked, "They are using an industrial spray, and a variable water heater. Is that correct?"

"That's fine," said John.

"How far should the sloping floor extend?"

John measured out an area. "Not very far, if the area is enclosed by doors. They need to be made of glass to let the light in. We also need rails to place the towels on to dry."

"Yes. These were the requirements for the human diplomats also, which we have on record. However they requested separate shower rooms for males and females. Do you require that?"

"No," replied John, "we are mates."

Gwen laughed. "We shall shower together to save on water!"

Fred gravely said, "I am pleased to hear that."

John said, "We will have a meal, and freshen up. We will then need a discussion of what to do in the negotiations this afternoon. I'll tell you now that they will be willing to change the method of trading. They do not want anyone else shot. I feel that we should immediately secure what we call an 'agreement in principle' on this, and also as fast as possible secure an agreement on a method of arbitration which will work. I will think about this while I am eating. I will see you in an hour, as I also need a bit of a rest. Is this agreed?"

"Yes. We shall return in one hour. We shall discuss this among ourselves." With that Fred turned and went.

"Well let's get some food and sit down. I am exhausted," John said to Gwen.

In an hour a group of Waps including Fred arrived.

"We have discussed the developments so far and we are pleased. From your knowledge of human psychology do you guarantee that what you said will be the next development?" asked Fred.

"I can almost guarantee it," said John, "They will be more than willing to move over to a credit balance system, with arbitration over any disputes. Have you thought of what form the arbitration should take?" asked John.

"That is simple. We will have our own arbitrator, and the humans will have theirs. Our arbitrator will arbitrate disputes with us and the human arbitrator will arbitrate disputes with humans," replied Fred.

John smiled. "It is not so simple. The human arbitrator will be biased on behalf of the humans even though I am sure your arbitrator will honestly arbitrate on disputes with you," John said.

"Do you mean the human arbitrator will be dishonest?" asked the Waps. There was a buzzing sound among the other Waps.

"Slightly, yes. It is in the human arbitrators interest to be slightly biased in favor of his own species. I have thought hard about this. I think I can counteract this tendency, and force the humans to be totally honest," said John.

"How? By shooting them?" Fred asked.

John laughed. "We do not to need to be so drastic. We need to change the system slightly. We start by having a panel three arbitrators on each side. When an arbitrator is needed one side chooses one arbitrator from the panel of the arbitrators on the other side."

"Why will this work?" asked Fred.

"We will provide an economic incentive for the human arbitrators to be honest. They will get a fee for their services only if they are chosen. The human arbitrators will soon learn that to be chosen they have to please the other side as well as their own side."

There was humming among the Waps group.

"We can see that. But wouldn't that lead to a bias in the opposite direction?" asked Fred.

John replied, "Yes, but this is mitigated by my next suggestion. The choice of which side chooses an arbitrator is chosen randomly by some device. There is a one in two chance that one side or the other chooses an arbitrator. This should greatly reduce the probability of what we call a systematic bias."

There was further discussion. "Would not it be better to choose the arbitrators randomly?" Fred asked.

"No. In order to remove the element of bias against you, you need to retain the element of choice."

There was considerable humming.

"You are very clever. We agree with this proposal."

"Thank you. Our negotiations will proceed with that basis."

"And may I make a general observation," said John, "do not confuse logicality with cleverness. We humans would have not got so far by being stupid. I will go further to warn you that illogicality is not necessarily a defect."

There was further humming among the Waps participants. Fred replied, "Point taken. We will remember your warning."

"Well lets go in," John said.

They had arrived early, and sat there waiting. "I shall use this as an opportunity to calm myself. If they have a ploy to make me nervous it is not going to work," John thought to himself.

The human delegation arrived a few minutes later. The Chairman looked harassed. It was obvious that he had been under pressure in their absence.

John opened. "I take it you have discussed our proposals?"

The chairman did not look happy. He glanced from side to side. "Yes, we have."

"And what in general are your conclusions," John asked.

The Chairman coughed, hunched forward and said, "We are interested in your proposal to change the trading system."

John said, "Lets be clear about this. The proposal we are talking about is no longer shooting the traders, having a credit account on both sides against which the trades are credited and debited, and can be drawn on time to time at the request of either party, and any disputes go to arbitration."

"Yes, we are interested in these proposals," the Chairman replied.

John drew a breath, "They are all part of a single proposal. Before we go any further do you agree in principle to this proposal?"

There was silence. "We have a lot to discuss before we can agree," said the Chairman.

"We can discuss the details later. What we need is an agreement in principle before we proceed."

The Chairman looked at the Waps. "Do they need an agreement in principle?" he asked.

There was a humming sound. The Waps in the judge's chair said, "Yes we need an agreement in principle. And remember John is conducting these negotiations on our behalf until we stop him."

The Chairman said, "We agree in principle to these proposals."

There was a humming sound from the Waps, but John interjected, "Proposal. They are a single proposal. They logically stand together and the Waps wish to treat them as a single proposal."

The Chairman moved his cheek muscles. "This is being very restrictive."

"This is what the Waps want," John replied.

"Very well, a single proposal," said the Chairman.

"Thank you. Let that be duly noted."

"Now, the Waps wish to conceded the issue of the shooting of traders. That method is gone as far as the Waps are concerned, as long as you comply with the other requirements of this proposal. Our Waps negotiators are willing to discuss with your technical and banking people how to set up and operate the mutual credit accounts. However a possible stumbling block, which need not be, is the structure of arbitration." John rushed on. "For reasons of their own, and as you know, the Waps are very logical, they want the arbitration system to be as follows. As you can see that they have been very reasonable so far, I do not see why there should be irrational objections to their request."

John smiled. The human delegates looked at him suspiciously. "Each side must choose a panel of three permanent arbitrators. These arbitrators must be permanent, and replaced only on a two yearly basis. Replacement on incapacity or death must be dealt with in the details of the negotiations. The Waps would not be happy in such cases and will exact a penalty. Now, when a dispute occurs, and listen carefully, a random generator chooses which panel of arbitrators is to be chosen to hear the dispute. Then a representative on the opposing side chooses one of the arbitrators on the panel of the opposing species. That is the Waps requested arbitration system. Some of you may consider this system is overly complex, but the system is designed to reduce if not eliminate bias. The Waps do not like bias in arbitration in their business dealings. I am sure previous proposals have broken down on this arbitration process."

The Chairman said, "We will consider this complex process."

"It will be simple to operate," said John, "And it is far better than the present system."

"May we have this proposal in writing?" asked the Chairman.

"I shall ask the Waps," said John, turning to Fred.

There was a humming sound. "We will be happy to provide this proposal in writing," said Fred.

"In the Waps language," said John. The Chairman gave him a dirty look.

"And one other thing," John said. The delegates gave him a look. "The Waps are frustrated in their business dealings that they do not meet senior members of your major firms to negotiate on business deals. They are confined to negotiating with low-level intermediaries on the Line. As you are aware the Waps economy is large and complex, and the potential for trade is very much larger than what can be transferred over conveyor belts in these sheds. Senior members of the Waps commercial sector wish to meet senior members of major firms on the human side of the line, and vice versa, wish to invite senior members of your firms to meet theirs. This will involve a limited amount of travel of both species across the Line, visiting each other's offices to negotiate deals. Perhaps after we have dealt with the current matter satisfactorily we can go on to negotiate the details of these cross border visits and interactions." John smiled again and looked at the Chairman.

The Chairman mumbled, "We will consider that."

"There," thought John, "I have put you on the spot again."

They all rose and left the room.

"Progress," said John to the Waps, "One step at a time. And the offering a bit more to lock them into the agreement so far, and going on to the next step."

"Will this work?" asked the Waps.

"All locked in," said John, "Remember I have connected the concession on the executions to your arbitration proposal. They will haggle over details, and drag their feet; but it is, for the first issue, and partial visits on the second issue, what we call "all over Rover". Progress on military matters is tenuous at the best. The best I can do is get talks going. These military people and their negotiators like talking. I suggest that you keep them talking. You will gain something."

"We are very pleased," said Fred. "How long will the discussions go for?"

"For details, quite a long time. But for the executions I suggest that you suspend them right now. Inform them that you will suspend executions, if they will suspend executions, on the basis that negotiations be continued under the present conditions," John said. "That will put the human negotiators under greater pressure to succeed quickly."

Further humming and "We will do that."

Chapter Sixteen

Back at the apartment they found that their complete shopping list had been delivered already.

"How is this?" asked Gwen.

"Apparently Jack got some people to work for him, and they worked very fast," Fred replied.

They found that the shower had also been installed, complete with glass doors and a fan. "Heaven," said Gwen. "Where's the soap?"

After a joint shower, they unpacked everything that had been bought. "New clothing! Luxury!" said Gwen.

"Well, we had better make ourselves at home. We will be here for a while," said John.

"How long?" asked Gwen.

"As long as the negotiations last, at least," said John. "After that it will be up to the Waps. I hope they stick to their side of the bargain and not hand us over. How we can get away on the human side I don't know. We will have to get past the spaceport if we get that far. We will deal with that when we come to it. For the moment we will have to concentrate on being useful to the Waps, and hope that they will be suitably grateful."

The next day was almost a repeat of the previous day, except that a number of persons on the table had been changed. Also the number of people in the other rows had increased. The Chairman was the same, but looked as if he had not had much sleep.

John was carrying the script in Wasp language that had been requested the previous day. John had gone over a translation with the Waps, and had gone over the major details. As far as he could see that the system of arbitration prescribed by the Waps would work. He suggested one extra detail. The mechanism of the random selector. The Waps being coldly logical had just specified an electronic random number estimator, one side being odds, the other evens. John suggested that the humans would not be happy with that, and suggested something visible. Casting his mind back to a lottery device he had seen on a broadcast, he suggested a small glass dome containing equal numbers of black and white balls. A blast of air would churn up the balls, and a device would then rise through the balls and choose one ball.

"Why would humans want this complicated device?" asked Fred.

"Humans will never be completely happy with a selection system they do not see operate," replied John.

"I understand. We shall amend the script to provide for this," replied Fred.

When they walked in the room, they were as a consequence slightly late.

"I apologize for our late arrival. The process of writing our proposed requirements for the arbitration system delayed us. Here it is." He stood up and handed it over the Line directly to the Chairman.

"Thank you," said the Chairman, "we shall carefully study it." And he handed the script to a person behind him.

"We would also like to thank the Waps for suspending the agreement on executions," continued the Chairman.

"You are welcome," replied John, "but remember the system is just in abeyance. Any disputes from now on will have to wait for the arbitration system to be set up."

"We understand," said the Chairman.

"Now," said John, "my understanding is that we have made good progress. We have agreed to commence a system of arbitration of disputes instead of the system of executions," John stopped and made a face, the human delegation nodded, "we have agreed to set up a system of mutual credits; and I hope what we can discuss today is first setting up a sub-committee under the supervision of these negotiations to discuss the details of the arbitration system, and the mutual credits system. After that is done perhaps we can discuss the issue of persons crossing the line to negotiate deals on each other's territory. Is that satisfactory to you?"

"Yes", said the Chairman.

"Good. I suggest that we have two separate sub-committees, to speed these negotiations up. One a set of accounting specialists to discuss the operations and rules of the mutual accounting system. The second a sub-committee of arbitration specialists to discuss the arbitration system. We have made some progress on the arbitration system, so unless we have some fundamental disagreements on the mutual credit system we should make rapid progress. Is there agreement in principle on these two sub-committees so far?" asked John.

The Chairman had some discussion with the people around him at the table, and then said, "We agree."

"Good", said John. "Now are there separate locations on the Line where these sub-committee negotiations can take place?" He turned to Fred, "Do the Waps have any ideas?"

Fred hummed for a while, while the humans went into a huddle.

Fred spoke first, "While this court house is the only mutual public place on the line, on each side are the trading locations of certain long established firms. Alternatively, as this room is large it could be divided into three parts, and while our negotiations are conducted in the center separate negotiations can be conducted on each side."

"Which do you prefer, Fred?" asked John, thinking, "You're learning."

"We prefer the latter method. While the room will be crowded, it will allow us to communicate easily with out sub-committees. Also, while we are not greatly concerned, trading in these nearby locations will not be interrupted."

John turned to the Chairman. "The Waps prefer to conduct the other two sets of negotiations in this room. What is your preference?"

The Chairman looked relieved. "If that is possible that is our preference also."

"Fine, agreed," said John. "As space will be limited, I suggest that each sub-committee is confined to three members of each species. Also I suggest that the sub-committees operate on each side of us, and are separated from us by sound-reducing dividers that will reduce distractions. What do you think of these suggestions?"

The Chairman again conferred, and then said, "If the Waps are happy with that, we agree."

John turned to Fred, "Do you agree with that proposal?"

"We agree," said Fred.

"Finally, in regard to these subcommittees, when can they start negotiations? I am sure there will be certain logistical problems setting up the committees, so I suggest the morning day after tomorrow? Do you agree, Fred?

"We agree," replied Fred.

"And you Mr Chairman?"

"We agree," he replied.

"Well, that settles for the moment the issue of the method of negotiations of the credit accounts and the arbitration. Now, how do we discuss the possibility of members of each species visiting major firms on the other side of the line?"

John continued, "I do not think that these visits should be confined to negotiations on existing traded goods. They could include sales missions, and exchanges of information of what goods are valuable to ourselves that we think the other side may have available. Is not that correct?" and he turned to Fred.

"That is correct. We want an expanded commercial relationship."

"Perhaps we could now discuss an initial visit on both sides. But before we discuss that, I must point out that the possibilities of misunderstandings due to a simple visit is very large. Extreme care must be taken, and any dispute must be referred immediately to Arbitration. That will be one of the important roles of the arbitrators. We cannot allow a visit until an arbitration system is set up. Then short steps on either side. An initial carefully controlled and guarded visit across the street maybe. A getting to know you meeting, maybe with an exchange of information on most desired goods. Perhaps even, and I know electronic transmissions carry over the line, an exchange of communication devices."

The Chairman conferred with his colleagues. "Yes that sounds good."

John announced, "Well, we have covered a lot. Perhaps we can take a break now, and come back on the second hour this afternoon, to discuss this issue more."

The Chairman smiled, bowed from his seat and said. "Yes, we will see you on the second hour."

A more relaxed group entered the room on the second hour.

After sitting down, the Chairman asked, "In order to set up the arrangements for the sub committees, how will we discuss the arrangements between us?"

John answered, "I presume there is a contact person system if you previously wanted to arrange a meeting or a trial?" He turned to Fred.

"Yes, that is true. While no wires cross the Line, we have exchanged transmission devices. These are manned 24 hours. If the humans wish to contact us, they call us, and vice versa."

"Then I suggest that this method be continued. If the representatives discuss this matter, I am sure with good will, a mutually satisfactory system can be set up."

"I agree," said Fred.

"Yes, I am sure something can be set up," replied the Chairman.

"Further, after the three members on each side of the two sub-committees meet, I am sure that they can work out an agenda and the major issues. If they stall or fail to make progress, I am sure they can be replaced by new sub-committee members who will have an incentive to make fast progress," said John. He continued, "I am sure your side really wants this initiative to work," looking at the Chairman.

"Yes, we do," he replied, grimacing.

"Failure of the sub-committees to make progress, or to get bogged down on any issue, will mean that the discussions returned to this forum here. The Waps really want these initiatives to work. If there is insufficient progress of either of the sub-committees, in the opinion of the Waps, they have the right to pull back the negotiations to this main forum at any arbitrary moment," said John.

"We would like to specify a minimum period of negotiations by the sub-committees," said the Chairman.

"I cannot specify the level of the Waps patience, or indeed what they define as lack of progress," replied John, " I shall ask them if we should specify a set minimum of negotiations before taking over a sub-committees negotiations," turning to Fred.

There was extensive discussion on this among the Waps. Fred finally answered, "We would like the negotiations to continue without too much pressure. Our preference is that the sub committee negotiates up to 30 days without being interrupted. After 30 days, either side has the option of terminating the sub-committee negotiations and returning them to this forum."

The chairman turned to discuss the matter with the other members on the table. "We would prefer a longer period. 40 days," he said.

The Waps hummed. "We have already made a concession among ourselves. Our numbering for such a period is 27 days. We extended the period by three days to make it more convenient for you. As I said these negotiations can continue if useful progress is being made. If not it is better to terminate these negotiations at the earliest convenient time, and return the negotiations to this forum."

The Chairman discussed the matter again. "Very well, to allow good relations, we concede this point."

John said, "It is therefore agreed that the minimum negotiation period for the sub-committees is thirty days, and then at the option of either party the negotiations can be brought back to this forum." John grumbled to himself, "I hope this nit-picking does not continue."

"Right," said John. "The next item on the agenda. How are we going to manage these visits across the line? Now, Mr Chairman," he said, smiling, "I have been doing most of the talking so far. I would really like to hear what your suggestions are on this issue."

There were a few chuckles, and humming on his side. "Ahem," said the Chairman, picking ups some papers, "we have some preliminary recommendations." With that he began to read from the papers.

After he finished John turned to Fred. "What do you make of that?"

Fred and the whole group hummed and then said, "These suggestions sound reasonable, but matters have not been mentioned."

The negotiations then became a to and fro of detailed discussions, with an occasional interjection by John if there seemed to be a lack of understanding. "Thank God I can relax a bit and space out. Everybody seems to be having fun," he thought.

Time sped by. Eventually the Chairman smiled and said, "We seem to be making good progress. How about meeting again tomorrow?"

Fred answered, "We will."

John interjected. "Before we go, could I please raise the third issue? The military discussions. While I know it is certainly premature to even consider what each side wants or is going to say, could both sides at least turn their mind to how they would like these discussions to take place, that is, indeed if you want these discussions to take place."

The Chairman looked at him. "You are really pressuring us."

"Not at all. I just do not want the matter dropped and forgotten. Can we agree to discuss at the end of tomorrow's meeting how we would like to conduct these discussions?"

The Chairman looked at him. "I cannot promise anything. But if you raise the matter again we may perhaps discuss the matter of how the discussions could take place."

"I am happy with that. Are you Fred?" asked John.

Further humming. "Yes, we are happy with this progress."

That afternoon the discussions continued on the issue of the visits. By this time the main discussions were between the Waps leader and the Chairman, and were proceeding cordially.

Occasionally John interjected to keep things on the rails and to remove misunderstandings.

Finally they came to the question of which firm would be the first recipient of visitors. When the Chairman raised the name Albrecht & Co, John intervened and said that given the background of the current events, he felt that Albrecht & Co might have the wrong attitude to dealing with the Waps, and would think another firm would be more appropriate.

The Chairman went, "I do not think this this is necessarily so…" when Fred intervened, "We feel that our initial dealings should be with another firm."

The Chairman's face went grey and said, "I see. Well perhaps we can suggest another firm."

"What is the next name on the list?" asked John.

"The Consolidated Pharmaceutical Company."

"Yes," replied John quickly, "What do you think, Fred?"

"We are happy with that firm," replied Fred.

"Finally," said John quickly, "On the issue of the preparations for the military discussion, I note that all the feasible negotiation spaces are taken up by the other two sub-committees. As we consider these military discussions are not so urgent as the other two issues, I suggest that we wait for one set of negotiations by a sub-committee to be completed, and a military negotiation sub-committee can then take the vacated place. This is of course not to actually negotiate the military situation, but just talks on talks." John smiled.

The Chairman said, "We will consider your suggestion, and let you know tomorrow. Let us return tomorrow morning."

Afterwards John had a discussion with the Waps. "What do you think?"

"We are happy with this progress. But what are these talks on talks?"

"The humans as you can see are very reluctant to even begin military negotiations. They want to go slowly and carefully. They are aware that the structure of the negotiation process will have an effect on the negotiations. They want to carefully consider the structure of the negotiations."

"We understand. What do you think will be the outcome of these negotiations on the structure of the negotiations?" the Wasp asked.

"They will I think draw on the experience of other military negotiations among the human species. We have had many, as we have had many wars. It will be most likely be a large formal delegation, much larger and more formal than these commercial negotiations. As I am not familiar on the form these negotiations take I cannot advise you at present. I will try to check and gain information from various information sources. My guess is that physically the court buildings where we sit will be inadequate to hold all the persons to be present, as negotiators and advisors. You must be prepared to build a major facility to conduct these negotiations up the line. You will gain credit from the humans that after you have had discussion with the humans for two days, and the size of the requirements become known, that the Waps suggest that such a facility be built on the Line, well away from this town," John replied.

The Waps replied, "That is good advice. We thank you."

Chapter Seventeen

Over the next few days the negotiations proceeded apace. The sub-committees on each side commenced negotiations, and as John expected, the Arbitration negotiations finished first, along the lines John originally suggested, within the 30 days. The major firms were pressuring for a fast result. The military talks on talks started soon after, and as expected, there was a rapid decision to build a major negotiation center 50 kilometers to the north. That made all the negotiators very happy.

The accountants got stuck on basic incomprehension, and John was dragged in to assist. He was very terse with the humans and told them that after thirty days, if they continued to drag their feet, the negotiations would be taken out of their hands and returned to the main negotiation committee. The negotiators did not like that.

After interminable sorting through the issues John narrowed them down to two points of difference. First the Waps did not have separate banks as such, though they did have separate trading firms. All accounts were maintained at a central location. Second, strangely enough, despite their logic the Waps did not operate double entry book keeping, and operated a form of cash flow/asset-expensing accounting. "I suppose because the Waps are totally honest they never felt the need to watch one another," he thought.

"OK," John thought, "Compromises have to be made on both sides."

"First, the humans will be required to set up a single accounting body to deal directly with the Waps. The Banks won't like that, but that is tough for the Banks. They must be forced to do it. In return the Waps need to understand double entry book-keeping, so that they can operate it in conjunction with the humans' accounting structure."

He announced this to both sides. It was the humans who objected. The Waps were intrigued when they were informed that there was an improved accounting system possible.

"Right," said John. "You have twenty four hours to agree. Otherwise I am taking the matter to a higher level. Think about it. Or to be more precise, I want your superiors to seriously consider the matter overnight. I know that they are listening. The offer is simple. A single accounting body, in return for the Waps taking up double entry book keeping in the dealings with yourselves. Go! I will see you at the starting time tomorrow. This is the last chance for this sub-committee."

Sure enough, next day the human negotiators did not accept a single accounting body.

John said, "Very well. I invoke a return to the main negotiating committee. This sub-committee is terminated." And stood up and left, followed by the other Waps.

The next day they entered the area of the main negotiating committee and waited. Except for a few panicked faces peering at them nobody arrived. After half an hour John announced "We shall return at the same time tomorrow" and they left.

Sure enough the following day, there was the usual negotiating committee waiting for them with the usual chairman.

"Mr Chairman," John announced, "you know the main issues awaiting us. These are the sole obstruction between the human and the Waps trading under the new and improved system. These are, they bear repetition," and John was getting good at this, " two issues. One. There should be a single accounting body to handle the transactions between the Waps and the humans. Second. These accounts should be handled by the double entry accounting system."

John waited. The Chairman said nothing. John continued. "These issues are causing unnecessary delays. In return for your concession that there should be a single accounting body on each side, the Waps are willing to learn the human double entry accounting system, and apply it."

He turned to Fred. "I seek confirmation of this." Fred replied, "This is confirmed, given the solution to practical issues on how the two accounting bodies will communicate and transfer information, and the willingness of the humans to teach us how to operate your double entry accounting system."

The Chairman replied. "We are sorry for these delays. We are willing to concede that there should be only one accounting body communicating with your side. We are happy that you are going to use the double entry accounting system."

Fred announced, "We thank you. It is agreed."

John intervened and said, "There are very real technical issues. Can we set up a sub-committee again, this time with different persons, to discuss the most efficient method of the technical transfer of data between the two bodies? They can operate in the previous location."

"We agree," said the Chairman. "We agree," said Fred.

"Also as double entry book keeping is an alien concept to the Waps, they need to be educated on this. I would like you to select a person to be responsible for transferring this information to the Waps. An accounting educator. Now we are running out of space. But maybe this space in the center can be used as an education center," John suggested.

"We again agree. And may I say you keep coming up with bright ideas. You have been invaluable," said the Chairman smiling.

"We agree to both statements," said the senior Waps.

"Thank you," said John. "Just to force this along, can this technical sub-committee and the education committee meet at their respective places first thing tomorrow?"

"We will do our best," said the Chairman.

"We agree," said the Waps.

"Our trading is operating well. Your system of Arbitration operates well also. We have gone through the backlog of disputes and we are satisfied with the outcome. We are intrigued with the double entry book keeping. It is amazing how we have managed to operate so well without it. Technical contacts with the other side are going well, and we are both setting up a joint accounting system; connected due to your subsequent arrangements by a cable across the Line attached to one wall of the Court. The visits over the Line have gone well, and we have gained good relations with many individual humans with profitable result. And finally on the military negotiations the humans are happy with your suggestion and we are building a negotiation facility to the north of the town," said Fred.

"I am happy that you are happy," said John, "is that all you want me to do?"

Fred replied, "There is a lot more you can do for us. The list seems to grow. But we are coming to the end of your originally specified six months, and we have covered the main elements of our three major requests."

"Remember your promise that you will eventually return us to human society in a manner which reduces our chance of getting caught," John answered.

Gwen interjected, "Yes. While I am happy to be here, I do not find our living conditions really comfortable."

Fred replied, "I am sorry about that. However we are very happy with this outcome. You have gained major credit with us. More than enough to bear the cost of us returning you to your society."

"However," he continued, "the method we are considering to return you has a problem. It is from our point of view secret. We do not want the humans learn of it."

John thought, then replied. "Well, you have not told me much at the moment. But consider this. First if you return us in such a manner that the humans do not know we have returned, it is in our interest to remain undetected. If we are not caught we will not be questioned. So your secret will remain a secret."

"Second, if you do not inform us of the details of this secret method, if we are caught we will not be able to provide the humans useful information. So your secret will remain a secret."

Fred hummed a bit. "But what if you decide to voluntarily tell the humans that you have returned, and the secret of the method of your return, out of loyalty to your species?"

John replied, "I refer to my second answer. Even if I voluntarily informed the humans of our return, and there was a secret method to return me, if you do not tell me what the method is, or keep the details secret, all the humans will know that the Waps have a secret method to return us. That may alarm them, but there is little they could do."

Fred hummed a bit. "We will inform you of our decision."

"However," Fred continued, "on this matter, I have to pass on a communication from your people. They are also very pleased with your services, and they offer you the opportunity of returning to your side of the line, and they promise that they will not harm you."

"No way!" interjected Gwen.

John said, "The instincts of the females of our species are usually correct. We will not put ourselves in the hands of these people. They will immediately extract everything we know from our brains, and leave us as idiots. They will claim that they have not killed us or harmed us. We prefer to return using your method."

"I will let you know our decision," said Fred, and left.

"What do you think of that?" asked Gwen.

"We are not off the hook yet. We have just to wait and see," replied John.

Chapter Eighteen

"Before you say anything, can we pass a warning on to Jack," John said to Fred when he appeared next day.

"What warning is this?" asked Fred.

"Since the negotiations have ceased, he is in an extremely dangerous position. He must cease trading and leave the planet immediately, taking his gains with him," replied John.

Fred hummed a bit, and said, "You will have to see him yourself. We have a different concern. He has accumulated a very large credit that he has not drawn on. To liquidate it will cause serious dislocation in the gold supply. It must be done over several days."

"I understand. I will see him, and persuade him that now is the time to go," replied John.

John and Gwen faced Jack the same day. "You have made quite a name for yourself. Famous galaxy-wide! When are you coming back?" asked Fred.

"We are not," replied John, "but I am here to warn you."

"Oh?"

"Your life is in danger."

"What! I have not done anything wrong or illegal. I am just making piles of money."

"If you hope to enjoy it you must get out now. Negotiations have ceased. You are no longer protected by the Waps, and the big firms will soon realize it. They want the milk supply business, and shortly they will get it. You must draw gold from the Waps, pay it into your bank account, and then do a quick flit. And I mean quick. Maybe even hire a private ship to get you out. You can arrange that while you are drawing down the gold. The Waps will only allow you to draw down a limited amount each day. Get security men to transfer it to your bank. At the same time arrange your exit as quietly as possible. You may be able to draw on the money in your bank from another planet."

"Are you telling me to cease trading?" asked Jack.

"Yup. Tell the Waps when you are going to cease trading so that they can arrange an alternative supply. Then get out like a bat out of hell. Let nothing stop you. If you grasp after the last kilo of gold, it will kill you. You must get out now, as soon as the Waps have arranged an alternative supplier. You don't have to draw down the entire Waps credit, as they are perfectly honest. But go you must, if you want to keep your skin," replied John.

They left Jack in a very pale state.

"We have informed Jack to leave as soon as he has transferred the milk dealing to someone else. I don't know whether he will accept our advice," John informed Fred on his return.

"Understood. We will monitor the situation. I have of course heard what you said to Jack. As he has been valuable to us, we do not wish him to die. But if you feel the humans will kill him, it is best for him to go to a safer place," replied Fred.

"Now we have discussed among ourselves your transfer to human society," continued Fred. "If you undertake not to disclose yourself to your people, and if apprehended, what knowledge you have of the method of your secret transfer, we will transfer you to your people," Fred continued.

"I promise never to voluntarily inform the humans of your secret transfer', John said. He nudged Gwen, "I do too. I promise."

"Good. Your transfer will be by spaceship," said Fred.

"But…but…how? The 'Pinch' is completely closed off. I know any one of your spaceships could never get by our cordon. The worm hole is blocked."

"Do you want to know? The knowledge will cost you a certain amount of credit," replied Fred.

"Will it prevent our transfer?" asked John.

"No."

"How much credit will it cost us to be told?"

There was a mumming sound. "One hundred kilograms of gold. We have given you a reduced price as we feel that at a later date it may be necessary for you know this information," replied Fred.

"How much is our credit at the moment?" asked John.

"Three thousand two hundred and fifty kilograms, but your transfer will cost about one thousand kilograms. You will be landed with about two thousand kilograms."

"Fine. Tell us the minimum details to reassure us the transfer is minimally dangerous," John said, looking at Gwen.

"We have another wormhole leading into human territory which we sparingly use," replied Fred.

"I thought as much!" said John.

"Which planet will you drop us onto?" John continued.

"We do not know its name. We know humans inhabit it. We will land you in a lightly inhabited area near habitation. From there it will be up to you."

"Will you land us with adequate means of survival?"

"Aside from your gold, some food and clothing. We considered gravity packs, but rejected them, as we have no human ones. You will be landed within a day's walk of a small town. We also intend to leave a transmission device, with which you can call to be picked up by a spaceship if needed," said Fred.

"A possible escape? That is sensible. When do we go?"

"Now if you wish. Your task here is complete."

"Get me out of here!" shouted Gwen.

It was dark when they approached the space ship. It did not seem very large, but its size was difficult to see.

"We have prepared accommodation for you, more restricted in size than your present accommodation, but we have included a toilet and shower," said Fred.

"Oh, there was no need to include a shower!" said John, "as long as the trip is not too long."

"We did not know how necessary the shower is for you. From the reaction of your female companion, and the time she spent in it in your absence, it seemed that is very important." Gwen blushed.

"Fine," said John. He looked at Fred. "Is this the last I will be seeing of you?"

"For the present time. I will not accompany you. But if you cross over to Wasp space again I may see you."

John was then stuck for words. "Fred, Gwen and I owe you our lives. We are very grateful. In human psychology you have gained great credit with us. Almost without measure. Also, and I don't know if you understand human psychology, but I have grown very fond of you. Thank you very much for all you have done for us."

Gwen said, "Me too. Thank you very much, Fred."

Fred replied, "In our peoples' terms, I have grown very fond of you. And I am also very grateful for all you have done for us. It is possible that the gold you have earned underestimates the value of your services. You should have stayed," and there was again the strange chuckle.

At the spur of the moment John said, "I want to do something human friends do. Shake your hand. May I?" Without waiting for a reply, he sized on of the four hands in front of him and shook it. It was dry and hard, but Fred did not resist. Then Gwen said "Oh Fred!" and leapt forward and gave him a hug, placing her cheek on his thorax.

John's heart went to his mouth. There was silence, and then Fred replied, "Thank you for these signs of human affection. I will remember them with gratitude."

While the lift carried them to the airlock they looked down to see Fred looking up at them, the multiple lenses of his eyes reflecting the spaceport lights.

They were shown to their cabin, which was as Fred described small and cramped, but had all the facilities. "Stay here always," were the only terse instructions they received.

They soon felt the ship take off and shortly after that they felt the ship jump through the wormhole. "Out of the Pinch," John thought. They settled down, and several wormhole jumps occurred over the next ten days or so, John estimated.

Eventually the cabin door opened. "Your journey is nearly completed," said the Waps. "Are you ready to go?"

"Yes," said John. "Do we need any of these things?" pointing to the mess in the cabin.

"No," replied the Waps, "you have adequate supplies."

They were escorted to a small landing craft. There were two Waps standing there. One started talking. "You will be landed on the planet below. On top of a mountain about 10 kilometers from a small town. You will be landed at night. You will be left with two thousand two hundred and twenty kilos of gold, which we consider fair payment for your services after expenses. Do you agree to this amount?"

"I agree."

"You will be left with some food and clothing. Also the person you called Fred asked us to leave you the paper and disks you call money, which you gained from your first shopping expedition."

"I forgot about that! Please thank Fred for thinking about that."

"Finally we will leave you a transmission device, which will be hidden in a suitable location. When we are on the ground you will be instructed how it operates to summon a ship. The arrival will not be for several days, as a messenger device has to go through several wormholes. You will need to stay hidden for that length of time."

"How long will that be?" asked John.

"The vessel will land on the sixth night after you send the message."

"Understood."

"You both will also be given a transmission device which fits round your wrist. It resembles an ornament we have seen some of your species wear. You must wear it always. It will periodically stimulate your skin if we wish to contact you. You must then travel to the transmission device and activate the mechanism. And you will be picked up six nights later."

John said, "Is this likely to happen?"

"Only in dire emergency, and the need will be by both our species. Otherwise you will be left alone. Are there any other questions?"

"I just need a digging device to bury the gold. I cannot leave it on the surface on top of the mountain," said John.

There was a humming sound. "Such a device will be provided. As it is obviously an alien artifact, you must hide it after use. You will be instructed how to use it, as it is a multipurpose power tool," the Waps said. "Are you ready?"

They entered the craft. Two padded seats had obviously been prepared for them. They cast off and soon entered the planet's atmosphere.

Eventually there was a bump and the craft landed. The airlock opened. Strange scented air flooded in.

"Please leave," said the Waps. They got out. It was dark. The air smelt slightly damp and strangely scented. The gravity was a bit lighter than earth normal. The sky was overcast, but through the trees John could see lights of a town in the valley below. There was clanking behind them, and the gold and supplies was landed.

"Here is the transmission device," the Waps said, "If you need us just pull down that red handle." And he pointed to a handle constructed for human hands. "Where would you advise I should hide it?"

John looked around, and saw a tall conifer tree a short distance away. "Half way up that tree. No one will look up there or will see it from the ground. Do you have something to attach it with?"

The Waps and pilot conferred, and pulled out tools and metal strips from what was obviously a repair pack, together with grav packs. They seized the transmission device and flew it half way up the tree, attaching it securely above a fork of a branch."

"Good enough," thought John, "I will remember where it is."

He then turned to the Waps. "If you help me bury the gold, you can keep the digging device."

The Waps said "Understood." He picked up the device and before John could say anything, shoveled a large quantity of rock and soil aside.

"Gwen," he said, "can you please help me," and he picked up the bars of gold to place at the bottom of the hole. "Yes, Captain Silver," said Gwen. John did not understand the reference.

He left ten bars on the surface. "We will bury these under forest covering," he said. "We will be back if we can in a couple of days with transport."

"OK, the hole can be filled in," he said to the Waps.

After the Waps had departed, without even a farewell, John looked at the lights far below. "We had better hide the gold and get moving," he said to Gwen, reaching round her waist.

She turned to him, put her arms around his neck and looked in his eyes. "Before we do that, I want one thing," she said.

"What's that?"

"Sex."

www.ingramcontent.com/pod-product-compliance
Lightning Source LLC
Chambersburg PA
CBHW071943170626
46813CB00005B/1806